VIRGO

RISING

THE AFFLICTED

ZODIAC

BOOK 1

By **M.J. Marstens**

Copyright © 2019 M.J. Marstens

First edition

Cover design by G.C. Les

Edited by Whimsicalworks4u (After July 2019)

CONTENTS

AUTHOR'S NOTE

WARNING: This novel is intended for readers 18+. There is explicit language, sexual scenes with multiple partners, dominant/submissive themes, and threats made by men who think they are gods. . . I hope you enjoy!

NOTE: This is the first novel in the series and will end with unanswered questions and events.

VIII

DEDICATION

To Elizabeth, who apparently wanted to be called 'Beth' in the 4th grade. Thanks for your never-ending support.

You're my B.F.F.F.

A Sucker Mother Fucker Bleep.

I dedicate this work to you: our years of code names (*remember Scorpio?*) inspired me. I'll egg you and give you a soothing massage with ambient ocean sounds.

The only thing left to say is: *A llama?* He's supposed to be DEAD! Yeah, weird.

I love you.

By the black of the moon, you too shall all become dark. Cursed to roam your creation, reincarnating until you finally destroy it. Only the maiden rising from light can save you from becoming your shadow selves

PROLOGUE

SATURN

My breath hisses as it escapes through my mouth and I toss my head back, awash in the physical pleasure of pounding in and out of the woman sprawled underneath me. I pull her hips closer to the edge of the bed and continue my punishing pace. I like to enjoy myself a little before I feast. She's making mewling noises, urging me to get on with both our completions.

I'm about to grant her unspoken, but insistent, request when I feel a tickling sensation sweep across my neck. The hairs there instantly stand on end and my head whips up, sniffing the air and scanning the room. My gaze narrows in on the corner to my left, up near the ceiling; there is most certainly a presence there. I can sense it, if not make out its shape. The entity freezes and then starts dashing around the room. I try to follow it, without disengaging my dick from its current home.

After a second, I lose sight of it. The woman beneath me lets out a startled squeak, and I realize I have stopped fucking her completely. She looks up at me expectantly, and I immediately begin again. This time I do not mess around, and I start eating while I drive my cock deeper into her welcoming folds. I gently tug at the essence of her soul while I bring her to the brink of pleasure. I can feel my eyes bleed to red and my fangs punch through my gums, but the woman is oblivious in her bliss. I continue to consume her when I again feel a presence.

Disconcerted, I stop my evening repast to look around, but when I lift my head, I lock eyes on those of the woman, or rather, the entity- who is inside the woman. I had stopped eating, but my dick has a mind of its own and slides in and out of my dinner. My eyes never leave the entity's, and we are locked in a battle of wills. That is, until the woman reaches up to grab my elbows. I'm so astonished by the action, I actually lean forward, as the entity intended.

The movement causes me to drive my cock deeper into her wet warmth, and I see the entity's eyes roll back in the woman's head. A groan of pure ecstasy rushes from the woman's mouth, but I know it's the entity's. I let out a fierce growl when the legs wrap around my waist lock tighter, urging me on. I feel my anger rise, but also my lust. Fuck if the two have not always gone hand in hand for me. I literally snarl as I fuck her in earnest. Breathy, almost silent, moans escape the thing below me and I can feel the body coil tighter, a sure sign of an impending orgasm.

Those eyes are again gazing into mine, but there is no fear, only a helpless pleading for me to not stop. I bring her higher and higher and I hear a husky *yes* seep from her lips, seconds before she shatters around my cock. Unblinking eyes stare at me in awe, and I lose the battle between my rage and my desire, and as her body milks me, I come deep inside her. Even now I'm on edge, realizing that something has taken over my meal's body. Even the voice does not belong to the woman.

Spent, I feel my irritation spike again, and I wrap my hands around the woman's throat. The once passion-glazed eyes now fill with apprehension. About damn time. Obviously this thing does not know who it has fucked with—figuratively and literally. I squeeze, demanding an answer without speaking, but instead of giving me one, those eyes narrow to furious little slits and a hand reaches up to slap mine away.

I'm shocked at this reaction and actually release the possessed woman, who slowly raises herself up onto her elbows to peer more closely at my face. No one sees *me* without invitation. Or dying. I let that message roll over my facial expression and a sinister grin hikes up one side of my mouth, but my intentions are premature. I can feel the entity fading away. I grab the woman by the shoulders and

5

shake her rapidly to keep the other from retreating, but it's a lost cause. Staring intently into its eyes, I growl:

"I'll find you." The thing just lets out a throaty laugh.

"You can try," it whispers before blinking out of existence. Fuck, my worst nightmare has come back to haunt me again.

CHAPTER 1

ZAHRA

"I'll find you."

The deep, almost decadent voice stirs me from my sleep. The recurring dream, or maybe nightmare, has been on a constant loop in my head since that night. Even now, weeks later, I still feel the flutter of fear in my chest at that sentence. And no small amount of desire. How can something so utterly terrifying be such a turn-on? Clearly, I need my head checked.

Again.

Laughing at my mental antics, I spring from the bed and pad over to the mirror. My brownish-blond hair (it's confused as to which color it wants to be) is in complete disarray and my cheeks are flushed from slumber. I chance a look out my window.

Yep, still winter.

Outside, the world is white, glittering, and shiver inducing. The thermometer on my window reads 'butt-ass cold'. Okay, it doesn't actually say that. . . It doesn't say anything because it's not even digital. Out here in the boondocks, good ol' mercury thermometers still tell farmers and country folk how miserably cold it's. But in a few weeks, the snow *might* melt and the earth *might* thaw enough for a few early spring plants to poke out of the ground. Or the snow might linger until past Easter, making egg hunting a joke in the bleached outdoors.

Welcome to the Himalayas! (a.k.a. northern Minnesota, eh.)

Realizing that another six to eight inches of snow fell overnight (atop the already existing fourteen) makes me glad I'm currently jobless. My gran always told me to find the silver lining in every situation and that's mine for this one-because surely if I had a job, I wouldn't be going to it today anyway. Speaking of no current income flow, I boot up my ancient laptop (still sporting Windows XP, woot-woot!) to check the most recent job demands filling my inbox.

If they are similar to yesterday's and the day before that's and the day before that's. . . well, I'll be breezing onto breakfast and book binging soon enough. Just as soon as the internet gets going-yay, Ethernet! (I was promised high-speed wireless last fall from the county, but either they haven't made it out to my neck of the woods yet, or. . . I'm not getting it. But some pipe dreams never die.)

While I wait, I inhale deeply from my steaming cup of detox tea and the exhale a disgusted breath. It smells as bad as it tastes- but anything with the word 'detox' is bound to offend all taste buds, right? Dutifully drinking (why I'm making myself imbibe this stuff- oh yes, it was recommended on Dr. Oz last month. Thank you, Doc.), I scan my email, visually assessing my inbox. Three quarters of it's junk. . .

Why do I even have a spam box?

Only three are from prospective employers. Two are from China, begging me to join the amazing teaching opportunities for English speakers. Is China warmer? Something to seriously consider at this point. But it's the third one that has me giving a small shriek of joy, seeing the beautifully scripted 'M' next to the envelope icon that is begging to be opened.

See, earlier in the week, I was applying to teach at various retreat centers and came across a job post at Indeed.com for a metaphysical specialist- specifically someone who has skills in astrology, tarot, numerology, and energy healing. It's like the position was *made* for me. Add to that the job was at one of the swankiest resorts in Tucson, AZ *and* started at $73,000 a year- well, I'd take that without blinking and never think of this snow-forsaken state again.

Sorry mom and dad.

But honestly, my skills are wasted in this icy hellhole. Snowmen don't pay to have their natal chart read (even if you make them one). That hint of mental instability has me cracking another grin. Boredom can make you do funny things. Add being stuck in this house for the past nine days and I thank god that I haven't started looking into Snowmen transits. (It's not going to be good- the sun's going into Aries and I'm not sure their cold personalities can take that much fire. I foresee some definite squares in their futures.)

I refocus on the task at hand.

Email.

Reading.

Potential celebrating of job invitation.

Yes!

Before I can get ahead of myself, again, I digest the words in front of me. Better to have actual confirmation than to think I do, right? Greetings are offered to me from sunny Arizona (*are they rubbing it in?!*) and thanks for submitting my job application and resume to Miraval Resort. It sounds so mechanical and distancing that I almost stop reading. I know these emails, generic send-outs thanking you for your interest but declining it otherwise. Yet I force myself to continue to the second paragraph and I'm rewarded with the words 'passed our initial assessment'. Heart beating, I scan the words 'phone interview' and 'in-person interview'.

Holy shit, holy shit, holy shit!

Baring nothing goes awry with the phone interview, they want me to come in for a one-on-one interview at the resort- all expenses paid!

I think I must have blacked out, because when I finally focus on what's in front of me, my tea is cold, my computer screen is black, and my legs are numb from having sat on them for too long. Maybe I'm just in shock. This seems like a dream come true... I mean, even if I don't get the job, I get a mini vacation out of it, right? Silver linings. It's time to make this a go. I groan, realizing that my computer has run out of juice and electricity is really hit and miss these days.

Due to weather, not lack of paying the electric bill, thank you very much.

Okay- it might be the latter, but the former is definitely giving a running for its money.

I decide I'm going to need to go into town. The library has free Wi-Fi and I can mooch off their electricity and charge my computer up at the same time. Also, my phone, tablet, and iPod.

Don't judge me.

But getting to town is going to be a battle. I'm pretty sure my car won't run even if I do manage to unbury it. Good thing I have friends! I text Edgar to see if he'll come pick me up when he passes my house. Edgar works for the county as a snow plower. He gets paid a butt-ton of money, has three months off a year, and dental. . .

He also has to be on call at all times during snow storms (a.k.a. every other day for four months) and works in freezing conditions, having to get out of the plow from time to time. So, I passed on that job, but bully for him, it seems to be working out in his favor.

I turn on my phone, send him a text, and then quickly turn it off again. I wonder if all this on/off action runs my cell battery down even more. . . something to Google later. After about ten minutes, I turn my phone back on and smile at the envelope dancing in the upper left-hand corner of my phone screen. It says that he's clearing out back roads about five miles from me, but might have to help dig out Old Man Pearson's tractor before continuing his route.

Estimated arrival time: two hours.

Yep, two hours for five miles.

Well, that would give me plenty of time to shower, redress in my pajamas and pack my stuff up. I make a grocery list while I'm at it- two birds and all that. I do have some money, but it's dwindling fast. My parents were in a car accident two winters ago coming home from Chicago. Icy roads and no close hospitals. A lump rises up in my throat. I had been in Mississippi, finishing my master's degree. I rushed home immediately, but not soon enough. My mom and dad both died en route. Having never had that closure, it feels as if a constant hole is yawning inside my chest, my heart completely missing.

My parents left me everything, including my childhood house. No siblings meant no battling an attorney about the will. More silver linings, right? Both my mom and dad were tenured professors and had money in their savings. I finished my degree up here (thank you University of Southern Mississippi!), which was a miracle of god, considering I could barely focus on anything beyond my loss.

Honestly, I think the school just threw me a pity bone and being the class-act my parents raised me to be, I took it slobbering everywhere. I think the cold winter helped freeze the worst of my despair and grief, but come spring, nothing unthawed. I remained numb. I shut out everyone, even my closest friend (she lives in Chicago and the connection is too much to bear). I was simply a robot working on autopilot.

That is until this past November, whilst mindlessly Cyber Monday shopping (I don't know who made this day up. . . but I hate them and simultaneously love them- Black Friday shopping without ever leaving the house. . . Seriously, only an evil genius could have done this), I realized I only had a little under $10,000 in my account. While that sounds not-so-bad, I pay nearly $2,000 a month in bills.

Student loans. . . like herpes, that shit just keeps following you everywhere.

Knowing I would be out on my ass come March, I started using the fireplace and lighting a lot of candles. I also started trying to build an online clientele for my astrology and numerology business. I bet you didn't know they had master's degrees in those, huh? That's because they don't. Like 90% of every other college graduate, I don't use my college degree. But I plan to, someday...

In the meantime, I have been reading natal charts, tracking transits and solar returns, and doing tarot spreads since I was fourteen. I made a pretty penny in college, too.

Drunk people were way more spiritually open and college campuses had those in spades. (Drunk people, not spiritual openness.) Unfortunately, my small town filled with obstinate, religious dogma did not want anything to do with my 'craft'. Sheesh, you threaten to curse someone once in your youth and that crap will haunt you forever.

People don't forget. Not in a town of five hundred.

My parents commuted to work about an hour away, but this weather makes me cringe just thinking about it, let alone driving in it. I might have grown up here, but eight years in the south has made me soft-bellied. (Metaphorically- not physically. Physically, I'm a brick house of abs. Alright, that might be a slight over exaggeration, but I also didn't pack on the weight like so many other college goers.)

I figured that this is why the internet was invented- so lazy people like me could do their work and never leave home...

Or shower...

Or get dressed...

Or even get out of bed.

What I didn't know: everyone wants to work from their beds naked- hence the eighty thousand online astrologists, numerologists, and tarot readers.

Getting my foot in has proved nearly impossible. Until today. Today might be the first sunny day I have had in two years.

CHAPTER 2

ZAHRA

I get ready and wait for Edgar. My duffle bag looks like I'm having a sleepover at the library, but everything I own has a different cord and charger. . . technology, right? In the distance, I see snow shooting skyward at a brisk pace and my heart rate spikes up in anticipation. Edgar is almost here! I'm finally about to get out of this house!

When my folks first passed, I don't think I left the house for nearly two months. Now, I go a little stir crazy even thinking about that time in my life, but again- I was running on autopilot. Nothing like your survival skills giving you a kick in the gut to motivate you. Either you have money to pay the bills and eat. . . or you don't. And those student loan sharks are aggressive as hell! Those fuckers wouldn't even cut me a break after my parents passed and I ran out of forbearance.

Twatwaffles.

I hope karma bites them in their asses.

(Also, please do not ask me what a twatwaffle is, as I myself really do not have an idea. I read it in a novel once and like the way it sounded. Therefore, I can only hope I'm using the word accurately. Again, there is no need for judgement.)

The blinking lights of the snow plow crest over the hill and I trudge outside to meet my sturdy limousine. And when I say 'trudge', I mean literally. . . like feet sinking knee deep in snow, lifting said feet out, and repeating. I miss you, eternally warm state of Mississippi. When I finally make it to the snow beast, Edgar is already out and opening the door to the cab. What a gentleman- and I mean that. Not a lot of guys today would come to pick you up to chauffeur you into town and open the door for you. . .

Oh- and bring you chocolate donuts (I sat on them first, but they eat the same).

Sometimes I really wish Edgar was dating material. Regrettably for us both, I don't feel the spark- but damned if he doesn't continue to try. Brownie points for him. (Oh, and FYI, I have never led this boy on- not once. . .

Except for that one time.

When I really wanted to go see that concert.

But other than that, I have been very upfront about my interest- or lack thereof.

Unfortunately, Edgar did not seem to get my 'just friends' memo. Making out with him that one time might have also blurred the lines. Grief can make you do funny things. (And there is really no need to point out that I *may* have allowed the situation to become misconstrued on his end. I'm working on it.)

"Hey, Gorgeous! Glad I could come pick you up. Wanna go out to eat tomorrow night?"

A free meal?

"Sure!"

Fuck, so much for working on it.

Okay, I'm going to try harder- later.

Scouts honor.

Edgar and I make small talk while driving into town. The library is really only a five-minute drive from my house, but with the roads all iced over, it takes closer to ten. Even in a plow. Edgar's hand keeps brushing mine which is resting on the center console. I quickly deter him by shoving it inside the donut bag and stuffing my face. Really lady-like, but I'm hoping it turns him off. . .

Judging by the look on his face, he's more impressed than repulsed by my ability to hork down four donuts in three bites.

I cannot catch a break.

When we finally pull into the library (which is miraculously open, thanks to Edgar's awesome plowing), I lean over the council and give him a quick hug, before hopping out and scurrying inside.

"Text me if you need a ride home?" He yells.

I'm already half-way inside the building and give him a thumbs up. Wearing a dopey grin of happiness, he rolls the window up and drives off. Damn, he looked way too happy about potentially picking me up later. I really need to address the 'just friends' thing. . . but I'm putting it on the back burner for now.

I walk over and sign-in to take the only study room (not the only one available. . . the only one in general) so I have a semblance of privacy. Phone calls here are frowned upon. They *actually* kick you out of the library if you make one. It might have happened to me once or twice (maybe more). . .

I'm kind of surprised I'm welcome here.

(I also notoriously run up their electricity bill, but there is no sign limiting how many electronics you can have plugged in at one time. . . five might be a tad much.)

So, to not get in trouble by Head Librarian Grinch (not her actual title), I take all my phone calls in the study room. I think that is both fair and generous of me considering the temperature is in the single digits. Besides, it's one in the afternoon- no one is here studying anyway.

"Good Morning, Mrs. Gerty! What is the Wi-Fi password again, please?"

I try to sound as chipper and none-rule breaking as possible. Mrs. Gerty is not buying my shit, if her thinning lips and narrowing eyes are any indication.

"You asked that last time."

"Uh. . . um-" She cuts off my floundering.

"And the time before that."

"That is because I'm not trying to take advantage of the system! I want you to know I'm only using the library Wi-Fi *at the library*."

I say this like I'm scandalized that someone might steal the library's internet. For the record, I'm not. But only because I'm too far out of reach. She scribbles the password on a sticky note and hands it to me acerbically.

"Remember, there is a two-hour limit for the study room!"

I nod sagely, like I'm taking her warning seriously, but she already knows I know the loop holes in this joint. Yes, there is a two-hour limit, but if no one else reserves the room within thirty minutes, then I can go sign back in and she can't do squat.

Or I'll complain to the city council.

There is a war brewing in this town between Mrs. Gerty and the council. Chances are Mrs. Gerty will win, but there are eight other old and set-in-their-ways council members who will put up a good fight first.

CHAPTER 3

ZAHRA

I quickly get into the room and shut the door and tuck myself away from the small door window so she can't see me. Mrs. Gerty is much taller than my petite 5"2', but she still isn't tall enough to see inside and around the corner to spy on me. And the door has a lock. Silver linings.

Unzipping my bag, I take out my devices and their chargers. . .

And an extension cord with a power strip.

I get everything hooked up and predictably, the lights slightly dim at the power surge. Mrs. Gerty is no spring chicken, but she isn't stupid either. By now she has made a connection between me and the electrical anomalies, but I feign ignorance any time she gives me a pointed look.

I get my computer up and running and load my gmail. I pull up the Miraval job email and respond by asking when a good day and time would be to set up the phone interview. Almost immediately I get a response.

Is 2:00 today ok?

Perfect, I respond.

That gives me an hour to kill and an hour to talk before I have to get out due to my allotted study room time. Hopefully the interview will not extend past sixty minutes. I fiddle around on my computer and download some new stories to my kindle. I love perusing the erotica section. You never know what people are going to think up and write these days. . . pair it with some raunchy sex and you've got a best seller.

After I get nine new books, I then make a list of everything I want to read that is not covered under Kindle Unlimited. My list totals eighteen books. I slip out of the room and to the front desk and set twenty-seven books on the counter (they are part of the reason for the bulging duffle bag). Mrs. Gerty glances up from the computer and kind of sighs when I hand her the list.

See, at our library, we have an inter-library system where libraries from all over the state and even the country can share books with each other. Apparently only *the most prestigious* libraries have this feature. Why our small town book nook tries so hard is beyond me, but bless them. This library hasn't updated their stock since the sixties and I would be woefully lacking in reading material if not for inter-library loans. This program also costs a pretty dime and to keep funding it, the city council requires that a certain quota be met monthly.

I single-handedly outdo that number in a week.

That's another thing Mrs. Gerty is so sour about. She knows without me, she can kiss her prestige out the door. But damn if she doesn't want to shove me out the door and burn my list. When I first started requesting these books, I tried to keep them. . . normal. But after a while, I realized I could not afford my book addiction (that's a serious thing, people) and I needed to start borrowing more. The first few books on astrology and whatnot were popular items- if their due date slips were any indication, but Mrs. Gerty looked horrified when she saw them.

Devil's material is what she whispered under her breath.

Well, I'm no saint and thought her reaction was priceless. . .

And then it became a game to see how much I could shock her.

It came to a point when all my books were placed in an opaque bag and set apart from the other book loans- as if my books might contaminate the other reading material nearby. I think she started this after I ordered the *Kama Sutra.*

With pictures.

I smirk just thinking of it.

Anyway, I think she's wary of my book requests, but she dutifully takes the list and reaches under the desk to hand me my opaque bag of this week's requests.

Awww- this week's material is so bad that she has to hide the bag in order to not defile everything.

I thank her, grinning broadly, and start taking the books out of the bag to see what they are again. It has been two weeks since my last library visit and request. (No doubt the Grinch was delighted.) She certainly does not look delighted now. Her eyes are wide and she wildly looks around.

I roll my eyes.

There is literally no one here, save her and me, but appearances must be kept apparently. Feeling mischievous, I pull out one of the books from the middle, it's called *Fuck It: This is My Life.* Lifting it in the air, I ask her:

"Do you think they'll make a sequel to this ?"

Mrs. Gerty makes a choking sound and picks up the phone.

"Excuse me, I have to make an important phone call."

I wait until she walks to the front door before I let out a little laugh. I might be twenty-seven, but I could still act seven just fine. I get back to the study room and check the time. Fifteen till two.

Ok, time to get in the zone.

I'm not an overly anxious or nervous person, but I really, really, *really* want this phone interview to work out so I can go to Arizona.

Don't get me wrong, I really, really, *really* would love to have the job, but just to get out of here for a bit sounds divine.

And that requires a successful phone interview.

Good thing I'm clever, articulate, and can spin a yarn to get my way in almost any circumstance. (I also have perky boobs and a big ass, so if I'm dealing with men, I do not have to try as hard- sadly, but also to my benefit.) Clearly, these assets are of no use to me in a phone call and my brain and mouth are going to have to do all the work. Hopefully they can function together and not get me into trouble for once.

At 2:00, I take a deep breath and unplug my phone from the charger.

Go time.

27

Wait for it.

And. . . no call.

Another minute ticks by and still no ring. I'm a very prompt person, but I understand that different clocks might have different times and so I wait another five minutes. When no call is forthcoming, I check my email. The response I received today was so swift, I just assumed the phone call would be similar. There are no new emails, so I reread the old messages to make sure I had the right time. . . scanning email. . . . 2:00. . . . wtf?

Then it hits me- *2:00 Pacific time.*

Arizona is two hours behind us, so my interview will not be until 4:00.

Crap.

I had to be out of the study room at 3:00 and barring no one came in to use it, I couldn't get in again until 3:30. Hopefully there wouldn't be a large school rush today because of the weather (only in this state where four feet of snow falls overnight, do kids still have school the next day). Well, I still have an hour to kill and Ol' Gerty the Grinch is not kicking me out a minute before 3:00. I kick up my heels and get to reading on my computer.

At 3:00 *exactly* a brisk knock sounds at the door. I had gotten lost in my book and hastily now start unplugging cords and stuffing them in my duffle bag.

"I'll be right out. I'm just finishing this riveting paper on the science of pagan magic."

I hear an irritated huff and the shuffling of feet walking away.

Ha. I know precisely how to get her goat.

And how to buy me an extra hot second- which I don't waste because Mrs. Gerty is a menace hidden in an old lady's body. Quickly exiting, I find Mrs. Gerty standing not too far away. I smile and nod before heading to the backroom. It's like a living room, complete with a giant rug, armchairs, and a fireplace. I set my phone on a twenty-eight minute timer and pull out my grocery list to review. When the alarm begins vibrating in my lap (*not like that*), I make my way to the front to sign-in again to the study room, but Gerty Grinch's smug look gives me pause.

I look over and see that the door is closed. Sure enough, someone else snuck in- no doubt encouraged by that grouch. Tough luck for me. Surprisingly, the library has a small gaggle of kids and parents in the atrium and Mrs. Gerty refocuses herself to attend with them. With her attention diverted, I dart around the corner and up the back stairs to the second floor. I'll thwart her yet [insert evil laugh].

CHAPTER 4

ZAHRA

Let me take a second to describe my library to you. It's a lovely, two-story Victorian building- completely renovated. I wouldn't give Gerty Grump (I really like my alliterations where she's concerned) the satisfaction of knowing this, but this building *is* prestigious. It's timeless architecture in a time where everything else is modern. (Like the front reception area, where the study room was added, along with a row of computers and shelves of DVDs.) I adore classic architecture (also not my one of my college degrees). I most especially adore the crown molding in this place.

I take a moment to let my fingers trail across the detailed beadboard on the walls and look around at the rows of shelves. Everything looks and smells slightly musty. It's one of my favorite smells after petrichor: eau de bibliothèque. At first glance, the second floor is reminiscent of the library basement in the movie *Ghostbusters*.

Except not haunted.

Just shelf upon shelf of old and never-touched manuscripts.

Poor things.

I hike it to the farthest corner of the upper level, where the second-story restroom is located and enter. It's one of my favorite places in the entire library.

Don't laugh, I mean it.

There is a single stall, but the toilet is old fashioned, with the tank sitting high and a dangling handle for the flusher. A matching delicate, porcelain sink graces the corner, with an actual bar of homemade soap and a monogrammed hand towel (whose, I have no idea). The pièce de résistance is the big bay window straight ahead, outside of the stall. An admittedly odd thing to have in a bathroom, but it somehow works. I love to sit on the bench ledge and read. I like to lock myself in here for privacy, without having to sign-in. . .

Mrs. Gerty followed me up once and refused to leave until I came out. I don't know if she thought I was stealing books or what, but I had to pretend I had a bad case of the green apple splatters to make her go away. Except- she didn't and I came out red-faced (from embarrassment) and out of breath (from making farting noises), after which I promptly left. General Gerty won that skirmish. (And I'm still counting that as an alliteration because both words start with 'g'.)

She and I face off a lot, but I like to think deep down, she knows of my profound love for this building and my obvious adoration for books. And even though we are constantly at odds with one another, we are actually kindred spirits of the literary world, enjoying the written word in this cozy cocoon of old-time décor and outdated interior design. . .

Then I think of Grinch's face when I asked if there was a *Fuck It* sequel.

Nope, she definitely hates my guts.

I'm just a delusional, yet hopeful, twatwaffle.

(I really need to look that word up in the urban dictionary. . . mentally adding it to my Google list. . .) I doubt Mrs. Gerty would help me find its definition, but thinking of her face while asking it has me cracking up. Still chuckling, I set up shop on the bench ledge. I'm not worried about her coming up today as she never saw me go upstairs. I while away my remaining time with reading. So many series, so little time.

At 4:00 on the nose, my phone vibrates. I knew this person was prompt. I answer the phone in a normal-volumed voice. The central heating in this place sounds like someone left the TV on at the highest volume- on a static channel.

"Hello?"

"Hello, is Ms. Delsol available?" A warm and friendly voice asks.

"Speaking, but please call me Zahra."

"Zahra with a Spanish pronunciation?"

I almost blow the older sounding woman a kiss. She totally gets my name. Do you know how rare that is? It seems like people cannot say your name correctly unless it fits some societal profile of normalcy. For example, my best friend is Ember, but everyone calls her *Amber*. God, we are a pair with our unusual monikers- but how damn difficult is it to call someone by their correct name?

I have been called Zahra, with a hard 'z' and rhyming with Sarah. Or I'm just Sarah. See, my dad's grandpa was originally from Spain. So to go along with our extremely Spanish sounding last name (*Delsol* means 'of the sun'), my parents thought it suitable to give me an unpronounceable-by-Western-society name that I would forever be correcting. Oh- and did I mention I'm super white looking? That's right, I'm the *white* Zahra Delsol. (And its pronounced SAR, rhymes with *tar*- AH. The rolled 'r' is optional.)

"Yes, ma'am. Thank you for pronouncing it correctly."

"You're welcome, dear. Such a lovely, unique name. I'm Mary, and I'm the head coordinator here at Miraval for the board of CEOs."

"Nice to meet you. Thank you for taking an interest in my application."

"Ah well, yours has been the most well-rounded and coherent yet. I had almost lost hope. Let's begin. According to your resume, you have been practicing astrology for over a decade?"

"Yes, I started interpreting charts and doing tarot readings when I fourteen. In college, I actually made a side-profession of it," I hesitate. "How proficient are you in astrology?" I don't want to lose her in the technical jargon.

"Not overly." I nod like she can see me and prepare my 'types of charts' speech.

"So, I start with natal chart readings, this is a birth chart, which is basically an abstract picture of the heavens at your time of birth. Depending on the client, I then recommend doing a Secondary Direction reading. These are also called Progressed charts and show you how your natal chart has evolved for every year of your birth. I also use transits, which are the planets' current locations in the heavens compared to your natal chart and Solar Revolutions, which are done yearly at the time of a person's birthday in relation to their current location to get an idea of the year ahead. Of course, there is so much more I can do, but this is a basic outline of my services."

I hear Mary make a humming sound of approval and the sound of a pen scratching notes over paper.

"Very interesting and well explained. Although, I thought transits were general?"

"Oh, they are when the planets and asteroids are viewed at their present position in the sky above. It's when overlaid on a natal chart for comparison that transits become personal. For example, in a few weeks the sun will transit, or enter, into Aries breathing new life and vitality to our world. This general transit brings springtime and warmth. . . unless you're from where I live," I joke.

"Clemenston not exactly a warm place in Minnesota?" Mary queries.

"Well, I do not think there is any warm place in Minnesota in winter, but here in our neck of the woods, it's especially cold. One of last week's highs was -33. . . without the wind chill."

I hear her audibly shudder.

"Well, thank goodness you're coming here! Our Arizona sun will warm you right up!"

I forget to breathe for a second. What did she just say? This interview has not even reached the ten-minute mark and I'm already advancing to the in-person interview?! I do my impression of a happy dance inside the library bathroom and thank god no one can see me. I hear Mary clacking away at her keyboard and wait for her to continue.

"It looks like your closest airport is in International Falls. They have a flight leaving this Sunday at 1:00, arriving at 5:00 with no stop and returning on Thursday. Is this too soon, or do you want me to look into next weekend?"

It does seem a little rushed, but maybe she knows how badly I want to get out of here. . . and who am I to turn down a four-day stay in the Grand Canyon state? With my approval, she buys the airfare and schedules a company car to pick me up and take me to the resort. I have a 10:00 meeting Monday morning, but the rest of my stay is at my leisure and *on the house.*

Go ahead and reread those last three words.

I swear I'm grinning like the Cheshire Cat atop the Queen of Hearts' head. All I have to do is drive to Falls International Airport to board- which is the only potential glitch in this whole plan. But come hell or high snow, I'm determined to make it to Arizona. I ask if I need to bring anything.

"Yes, please bring examples of your services, such as sample charts, and be prepared to do a Tarot reading. I'm emailing over the confirmation reservation for your flight and your tickets to scan. If there are any problems, I'm forwarding my personal contact information. Please do not call the company number, but me directly. And I'll see you on Monday!"

"Thank you so much!" I squeak out before disconnecting.

Man, that lady is efficient. I bet she could take on the Head Grinch any day. I needed to recruit her to my side.

The Gert was going down. (Please ignore my idiotic ramblings, I'm in a state of shocked bliss and cannot be bothered to make sense.)

I check the time: 4:08.

I just nailed a phone interview in eight minutes.

Either I'm totally badass or the other applicants were really incompetent. Mary did allude to the latter, but I like to base my success on my badassness (which is very much a word).

CHAPTER 5

ZAHRA

I take a moment to text Edgar to see if he can come to pick me up. I send him a kiss emoji as an incentive to come back for me- not because I'm leading him on further. It's a friendly kiss emoji. Besides, how literally can someone take emojis? One is an actual pile of shit.

I rest my case.

Edgar writes back that he'll get me when the library closes, which is not until 6:00. He's out salting county roads due to drifting and icing. He also sends an emoji:

A throbbing heart.

That could be friendly, too, right?

I don't ponder on it further but grab one of my books from my duffle bag and settle myself on the 'reading ledge' of the bay window, the blinds tightly closed. I always bring a spare blanket and traveling pillow, and I look like a cat all curled up. The only light is the soft glow of the lamp next to the sink. The book is interesting, but full of scientific data, and I find myself drifting off, enveloped in warmth.

Like always, my dreams eventually coalesce into that same vivid, recurring nightmare. The rooms are different,

41

the women are different, but the man is the same. And I'm an invisible force, watching the scene unfold- like the world's creepiest voyeur. Because these scenes are definitely X-rated. The man always has his back to me and is screwing the brains out of some ridiculously good-looking woman. Then, as if he senses me, he focuses on where I'm. . . uh. . . hovering, I guess. And I freak out and start darting around the room.

Every.

Single.

Damn.

Time.

Because let me tell you something about this man- *I'm not sure he's one.*

I say 'man' because it has a penis and very clearly uses it like a human man, but that is where the resemblance ends. This guy is a freaking giant, like seven feet tall! His dark, inky hair spills down his back in a straight waterfall of black, and I'm a little jealous of it. His skin is a muted cranberry red, which off-sets his creepy-as-fuck red eyes, and there is a sickle tattoo over his left pectoral. Add in some fangs, a defined body that Channing Tatum would be envious of, and inhuman movements, well, it seems pretty damn obvious to me that he's some kind of vampire.

I mean, fangs, right?

Where was I?

Oh, yes, I'm freaking out because he found me.

I start ping-ponging around the room to hide and end up *inside* the woman. (The really good-looking one he's currently fucking.) As if that is not messed up enough, it's like I become one with this chick and whatever she feels, I feel. . . . and it feels fan*fucking*tastic. Every leisurely slam into her/my body lights up all my nerve endings in pleasure. This vampire/demon/monster guy is scary as hell, but he sure knows how to give it to a lady- and I use that term loosely.

Monster Man (another great alliteration on my part) seems to want to keep his distance, but I want to feel him on me, over me, deeper inside me. Manipulating the woman's body I'm inside of, I tighten my legs together and grab his elbows to pull him closer. Then, I always try and do something else to shock him. Today I reach out and touch one of his fangs. . .

Ouch!

Fuck!

Stupid woman's body listening to me inside her!

Those suckers are sharp. I look down at her cut finger and whimper. The man looks at me in disbelief and exasperation, like I'm the world's dumbest person. Honestly, I'm a little offended by that look. Narrowing his eyes, he picks up my (her) finger and gently licks the blood off and groans, as if it's a decadent treat.

Definitely a vampire.

I have never seen him be gentle, and I watch as he softly strokes the fingertip with his tongue, the rough surface causing tingles to erupt down my back. A low moan escapes my lips and he starts sucking a little harder on my finger. And, like the lady I'm obviously not, I start moaning louder. Monster Man starts bucking his hips in tandem with his finger licking and the entire experience is like sensory-overload. I mean, I don't know how this is possible, because it's a dream, but I swear I see this chick's gray matter when my eyes roll back in her head. No real-life fuck has ever been this good.

(Quick confession time: I fake all my orgasms. Don't be horrified, I'm the one getting gypped. The secret is to not be *too* over the top; subtlety is a forgotten art. I guess there's the question of why I even pretend, since the other person doesn't even deserve the pretense since they obviously can't get me off.

Oh, and another quick sidebar tangent: Who else is a little pissed that guys have to get off to procreate? Men literally have to enjoy the process to its fullest to perpetuate the species. Proof that god is a dude if there ever was any. I mean, where is the justice in that? And don't tell me that women have double the nerve endings *down there* than men have- it's little consolation.)

Sorry, back on topic:

I'm getting dream railed and enjoying the ever-living-fuck out it, because this guy screws like a champ.

I don't even care that it's not my body, the sensations are real (which is a weird thing to think, since it's a dream), and I ride the high of her/my/our orgasm. It bursts inside me out of nowhere and paints the room in sparkly, little cascades of light. I feel the woman's pussy convulse around the man, igniting his own completion, which he growls out against her neck like a heathen barbarian.

My breath is coming out in panting huffs and I wait for him to make eye contact again and deliver his famous line. Slowly, he lifts his head from the woman's heaving chest and looks into my eyes, but instead of his normal I'm-going-to-have-to-kill-you-now look, his eyes are smug and a sense of unease prickles through me. He looks decidedly wicked, as his mouth kicks up in an evil grin.

"Found you."

What.

The.

Fuck.

I mean, don't get me wrong, 'I'll find you' is a scary sentiment, but 'found you' is even scarier.

What in the hell does he mean?

I don't like this hot nightmare anymore. (Let's not point out that most people do not enjoy nightmares right now, please, because most are not getting excellently boned by a potential vampire.) My brain races for a way to extract myself from this situation and I feel my eyes light up with victory.

"Tapioca!" I yell through the woman's mouth.

Take that, Monster Man!

Except, he doesn't look defeated. . .

He looks puzzled.

"You know, *tapioca*, the safety word."

Again, no response.

I close my eyes and cross my arms. If he isn't going to play by the unspoken rules of kinky fuckery, then I'm waking up from this dream charade. I hear him puff an aggravated breath above the woman's head. How dare *he* feel annoyed. I look up and open my mouth to give him a right piece of my mind, when I feel the weightlessness of waking up. His eyes remain locked on mine as I slowly drift into consciousness. I faintly hear him say:

"Found you, at last."

The grim satisfaction in those four words jolts me fully awake.

Why does this suddenly seem less like a dream and more like a waking nightmare?

CHAPTER 6

SATURN

I bury my head in my hands, trying to make sixes and sevens of my most recent encounter with *her*. The woman who hijacks my meals and brings me untold pain and sorrow. And pleasure. She has always been cunning and conniving, but this. . . *innocent act*. . . is something new. She always did like her games. But I'll not be drawn in this time. No, this time, I'll remain impervious. And when she gives me the information I seek, I'll end her life by snapping her *innocent* little neck in two.

ZAHRA

I bolt upright, instantly wake, and fall gracelessly to the bathroom floor. . .

Of the library. . .

Where I have fallen asleep.

My dreams/nightmares are getting out-of-hand and are far too lucid for my comfort level. I quickly dig into my duffle bag and pull out a dream dictionary. I thought to ask for it a couple weeks ago when I realized this subconscious act was not going anywhere. Of course there is no entry for 'potential vampire that plows possessed model'. Dammit, couldn't these books give examples or something? The chiming of my phone brings me out of my mental rant. I have a notification. It's from the Clemenston Public Library and says they will be closing early due to a potential ice storm.

This was sent at 4:58; it's now 5:04.

I move in a flurry of activity, throwing everything I own back into my duffle bag and sending a quick text to Edgar explaining the situation. Then I head for the door. I literally cringe to think about what Mrs. Gerty is going to say when she sees that I'm still here, but what choice do I have? I exit the bathroom and walk swiftly to the carpeted stairs across the room. Everything is now dark, except for the emergency lights.

Remember when I said this place was like the *Ghostbusters'* library, but not haunted?

That is because I have never seen it at night- alone.

I stop walking. Everything is encased with eerie shadows and darkness. The stairs I used to get up here are the closest to the front door, but also have no lighting. What if something is there, waiting? More logically, what if I fall and break my leg? I promise you Mrs. Gerty will not call for help.

Insufferable bitch.

I book it to the back, where there is an open wooden staircase lined with windows and more lighting.

Time: 5:06.

I walk down the creaky old stairs. For sure Mrs. Gerty has to know someone is here. I just hope she isn't within her rights to take me out with a fire extinguisher. As I round the corner, no lights are on down below either, save for the soft glow of a lamp in the library's back office. My heart starts racing in unease. . .

What if the Gerty turned into a monster and is now eating crickets á là *The Girl Who Cried Monster?* (I might have read a lot of *Goosebumps* in my not-so-distant youth.)

My dream/nightmares fuel my nervousness. Monsters have infiltrated my subconscious, but I won't let those fuckers rule my waking life!

I let out a pitiful war cry and strut boldly to the office. I wrench open the door and find. . . .

Nothing.

Oh, thank god!

I collapse on the floor- I'm not cut out for this kind of intrigue.

Knowing it's time to face the piper, I softly begin calling out Mrs. Gerty's name. I don't yell, because even after hours, that old bat will give me a dressing down. I walk to the front reception area and out to the atrium. . .

To the locked front door.

Son-of-a-bitch!

Here I'm worried about monster librarians and that woman has locked me in! (There really is no need to point out she had no clue. Just allow me to continue hating on her. Thank you.)

Now I'm in a quandary.

How the hell am I going to get out?

I don't want to stay here overnight. This is the *perfect* place for a potential vampire to come and kill me.

Sighing in resignation, I text Edgar again, this time explaining the new situation. His response:

Hold tight!

This is accompanied with a bouquet of flowers.

Shit, I just gave him the perfect situation to be my silver knight on a horse. . . .

Or is it my knight on a silver horse?

It doesn't matter because his plow is orange and it could be rainbow polka-dotted for all I care, as long as he somehow gets me out of this tangle. Is 'thank you' a sufficient gesture of gratitude in this situation, or am I going to have to cross the friend line again? Honestly, there are only so many more times I can cross that line before there is no coming back on his end. He probably thinks we are already dating. . . I should check his Facebook status.

Facebook never lies.

As I wait in the atrium, curious to see how Edgar is going to 'save me', I realize that I'm starving. When did I eat last? In reflection, I don't think I did. All I ate today were Edgar's donuts and that detox tea from this morning. I didn't even finish the tea. It was even grosser cold. Maybe Edgar could run through the mini mart, since I'm not going grocery shopping now.

Speaking of the hero of unrequited love (his), Edgar pulls up to the front doors in a blaze of flashing lights. He jumps down from the plow and marches straight to the front doors. He's so purposeful, it almost takes my breath away-almost.

Is he going to break down the doors for me?

This guy has some seriously romantic notions. I see him raise a fist. . .

And drop down a handful of keys, as he simply unlocks the door.

Huh.

I did not see that coming.

He must see the questions in my eyes, because he says:

"Mrs. Gerty gave me a spare key so I could help out around the library. I have been fixing some faulty electrical outlets on the side of shoveling the walks and salting them in my free-time."

He smiles sheepishly.

"She's such a sweet lady. She always thanks me by making a batch of cookies or a pie, since I live alone."

Mrs. Gerty, *sweet?*

Now I have heard it all.

Let's hope she never finds out about Edgar's infatuation with me or he can kiss his treats adios. It genuinely baffles me how Edgar is not married. He's definitely a family type of guy, and I'm kind of surprised he's not married with two-point-five kids already. Maybe he's waiting for 'the one'?

I feel my stomach drop. . .

What if he thinks I'm *the one*?

I look over to Edgar, who has just finished relocking the door. He gallantly picks up my bag and walks me over to the passenger side of the plow. Nope, he's just a true gentleman- he definitely does not think I'm 'the one'. He helps me up inside and shuts the door. As it swings shut, I catch his look of adoration.

Fuck.

I'm in denial.

Later just became now, and I need to rectify this before I do some serious damage to one of the world's sweetest men.

"I have a job interview on Monday." I say out of nowhere.

"Awesome, congrats! Is it here in town or in another border town?"

I fiddle with my jacket zipper.

"It's in Arizona, actually."

He does an immediate double take.

"What?"

"My job interview is in Arizona. It's for a metaphysical specialist position at the Miraval Resort in Tucson."

I watch his shoulders drop. Why do I feel like such a bitch right now?

"Is there. . . is there someone, ah, there. . . that you're seeing?"

The question makes him shift uncomfortably in his seat.

Does '*no, not unless you count a vampire that haunts my dreams*' sound like a realistic answer?

"No. . . no. Honestly, it's the first place that has reached out to me from the hundreds of jobs I have applied for and is actually monetarily worth uprooting my life from here."

Also, it's in Arizona and I hate snow, but I didn't want to say that to someone who makes their living from plowing it. Clearly, you have to like the treacherous white puffs of frozen water to deal with it every day for half the year.

"When do you leave?"

"Well, I leave Sunday- but only for four days. I have an in-person interview."

"So you don't definitively have the job?"

He sounds a little more exuberant, which annoys me.

"Technically, no, but Mary, the head coordinator at the resort, basically told me I'm a shoo-in!"

I might be stretching Mary's words a bit, but I feel really good about my eight-minute interview with her. 'Oh' is Edgar's only response, and I feel like a meanie again. I reach over and take his hand and speak as truthfully as I can.

"I like you, Edgar, and I appreciate everything you have done for me, but I'm ready to finally move on. . . past my grief. And I cannot do that living here."

"So, you're breaking up with me?"

Wow.

One of us was seriously delusional, but I just didn't know which one. . .

"Uh. . . yeah, um, I think we need a break. I guess I didn't even realize how *serious* we even were. . . I kind of am still just numb inside."

This confession seems to get a reaction out of him.

"Of course! Please, you don't have to explain further. I get it."

Doubtful since both his parents didn't die in a car accident coupled with internal bleeding and hypothermia- but that response seems a little extreme.

"Ah, well, thank you. So, again, thanks for driving me home. . . and I might have to pass on tomorrow's dinner. I have to get packed and everything. I also have to undig my car and make sure it runs."

By now, we are pulling into my driveway and I have never been happier to get home.

"Ok, do you want me to take you to the air-"

"Nope! I mean, no thanks, I don't want to inconvenience you any. . . I appreciate it though. Stay warm, Edgar!"

I quickly shut the door, wave, and run inside.

I find the potential vampire and I have something in common:

We are both monsters.

CHAPTER 7

ZAHRA

Sunday finally comes. Two more nights of sexy-time nightmares have put me on edge. But I'm fully packed and ready to finally wear a tank top again.

Current temperature in Tucson: 76°

Clemenston's current temperature: 12°

(And that is considered a heatwave.)

I need to leave here at 10:00 to make sure I have plenty of time at the airport. It's only an hour drive, but I want to give me two for safety, and another hour for check-in. You can never be too early, but you can definitely be too late. Another little gem my Gran used to tell me. I look out my living room windows etched with ice and frost. My car is scraped clean and dug out. . . along with my driveway.

Edgar came by.

Damn.

How do I even begin to rectify that situation?

Another time, right now, I'm going on mini-vacation. I just wonder if there is any medication on the market, legal or otherwise, that would make me dreamless. I could really use a good night's sleep. I had planned to sleep on the plane, but what if I do something embarrassing in my sleep? I swear to God, I woke up coming the other night. I didn't even know women got wet dreams, but I was a sopping and quivering mess. And so damn horny, I made myself come another four times. At least I can get myself off. I miss Blue, though. . . that was my vibrator's name, due to its actual color. But I think I might have accidentally donated it to Goodwill. Some lucky bastard got to unpack that treasure. Or unlucky bastard, depending on how you would rate finding a used vibrator in a box of miscellaneous housewares. I should probably shop for a new one. . .

Sans vibrator, I pack my bags into my trunk and double check I have everything in my bookbag that I need for the interview.

Check.

Check.

Double check.

Good bye, Clemenston; hello, Tucson!

The drive is a breeze (surprisingly), and I take this as a good omen as I pass through airport security. Once finally ensconced inside the airport terminals where no one can go unless they have a plane ticket, I start doing a little window shopping. I decide I can splurge a little bit and reward myself for a successful phone interview. Maybe they sell vibrators somewhere. . . I'm thinking a red one this time.

NOT because Monster Man has a red penis.

I just think it would create a more stimulating visual.

Seeing nothing to buy, I wander over to the Business Class Lounge. The attendant is flirting with some airline stewardesses, so I decide to walk in and give it a peek. I have always heard how ritzy these places are, with a private lounging area, bar, and other amenities- like a free Wi-Fi hotspot. The darkened floor-to ceiling windows block any passersby from looking in but also creates an intimate setting inside. The lighting is low and black couches line the sitting area. Tinted glass dividers break up, what I presume, are other rooms of the lounge. Snooping around for the bathrooms (I like upscale toilets and privacy), I begin to weave around the glass panes. It's almost like being in a maze of mirrors.

Glad I'm not a bird, because I would never make it to another part.

I round one pane and look up in time to see my reflection in the other across from me. Behind me stretches a hall and in the glass, I see a flash of red skin and long black hair before it turns the corner. My heartbeat kicks up and for a second I'm frozen with indecision before I race down the hall after *him*. The intricate web of glass dividers actually leads me back out to the main sitting area, where I bump into a woman. She's dressed in a uniform and obviously works here.

"Are you alright, ma'am?"

"Did you just see a red man?" I blurt out, without thinking.

Shit, I need to work on my brain-to-mouth filter. The woman's eyes narrow and her mouth puckers in disdain.

"Do you mean a Native American man?" She asks haughtily.

"What? No! Are you racist?!"

Now she just looks confused. . . and a little worried. I realize now she thought I was being prejudiced- not literal, because who has red skin for real?

(Answer: my super white cousins who cannot tan. Only burn. They do not make an SPF high enough for those poor souls. By the end of every family reunion, they resemble human crabs.)

"No-n-n-no, ma'am. Of course not, I just. . ." She trails off, obviously at a loss of what to say in this awkward situation.

Trying to rectify the conversation, I say:

"I'm sorry. I thought I saw someone. . . come this way. . . and I meant red suit, not skin." She looks unassured by words.

"Yes, one of our business class members did just walk out before you, ah, burst out here. He was leaving to board his plane. And he was *not* wearing a red suit."

"Are you sure?"

"Can I see your boarding ticket, please?"

Fuck, that escalated quickly.

Can security detain you for asking crazy-person questions?

Can they detain you for sneaking into the business class lounge?

More things to Google.

"Actually, it's time for me to board my plane, too, so thanks. . . for your help. . . and I'll just be on my way!"

I do not give her time to stop me, but simply dart pass her and run down the terminal like my ass is on fire.

CHAPTER 8

ZAHRA

Once I reach my gate, I walk to the restrooms across from it. I enter the family one for a quick second of privacy. Looking in the mirror, I question my sanity. I *know* I saw something. I did- but logically, the thing from my dreams would not be at the airport because it's a figment of my messed-up subconscious. Maybe my grief over my parents' death is deeper than I thought; maybe I'm unconsciously creating an outlet to release it through my dreams. . . . a really fucked-up outlet. Shaking my head, I make a decision: if the dreams have not vanished in a week, I'm seeing a therapist.

I refuse to be ~~crazy~~ crazier.

I come out of the restroom and sit at my gate. My flight does not leave for a bit, but I think I have gotten into enough mischief for one day. I need this mini-vacation, so no more asking if anyone has seen a red-skinned man. Yeah, I definitely can see how the lounge attendant took that the wrong way, now. I hunker down in a seat, away from everyone (in case security is looking for me) and pull out my charts to review for the interview. It says 'Jane Doe' at the top, but they are actually my natal and progressed charts. It's not 'professional' to use your charts or a previous client's for demonstrative purposes, but I know my chart like the back of my hand. I figure I'll come across the most competent explaining it.

So, for those who do not know much about astrology, a chart is a wheel divided into twelve sections. There are twelve zodiac signs, each having thirty degrees to equal a three-hundred-and-sixty-degree circle. Everyone has every sign in their chart; some are more predominant than others, depending on where the planets are positioned, and which signs are on the house cusps. We are so much more than our sun sign, which is what Western newspapers, daily blog sites, and the like focus on for our horoscopes. We are every aspect of our birth chart, comprised of every sign.

There are ten planets in every chart: the Sun, Mercury, Venus, the Moon, Mars, Jupiter, Saturn, Uranus, Neptune, and Pluto. (There is no need to point out that the Sun, Moon, and Pluto (debatably) are not planets. This is *astrology*, not astronomy, and I did not make up the rules.) Where and how the planets are assembled in a person's natal chart tells me a lot about their collective energy. Planets can be grouped together or spread out, mostly on the left side or the right, or predominantly in the northern hemisphere or the southern one. Mine are fixated to the right (which brings interdependence and karma-reaping), but straddle both the upper and lower hemisphere, being mostly in the 5th and 7th houses. Only my moon and Venus are to the left.

I'm so engrossed in trying to find new meaning to my charts (different days, different moods, they all bring a fresh perspective to chart interpretation), that I don't realize someone is leaning over me looking at my charts, too. I stifle a gasp and rear back, almost back bending into the chair connected behind mine. He has sandy blonde hair, light blue eyes, a charming smile- and is currently eating up all my personal space.

"Sorry, I was reading and looked over and saw your... I don't know what, I guess, and it intrigued me."

He pulls back into his own seat and I relax a little. I don't know what to say. On the one hand, I want to be repulsed, but this man is devastatingly good-looking. Like, I have never seen a man this attractive- unless we count my crazy, subconscious hallucinations (and I might). But I also don't want to pander to the double standard of society where beauty is rewarded. A creep's a creep, no matter how well-defined his arms look.

"It's a natal chart for astrology, but I don't really appreciate you being in my space like this and leaning over me. It's rude."

I try to sound firm, but I kind of want to lick his skin. He looks like a surfer and I wonder if it tastes salty.

Shut up, hormones!

You're not invited to this party!

His face retains its carefree smile but something moves inside his eyes. I get the sensation that I know this man.

"Forgive me, us Calies aren't big on personal space. I forget this from time to time."

"Calies?"

"Californians. We are big on free love, equal rights for all life, and chasing the next big high- or wave, for me."

I guess I did have him pegged correctly, but his line seems delivered and full of hippy crap. Not every Californian is like this, and I think it's an excuse for his behavior.

"Right, well, here in Minnesota we like our personal space to be an arm's length radius around us." I state primly.

"Oh, in that case, I'm not sure I was actually in yours then," he teases me.

Smartass.

I know I'm tiny- there is no need to rub it in.

But I relent a smidge and give him a grin. He leans back in a bit when he sees my upturned lips and offers:

"I actually was wondering if you wanted to get a quick drink? Our flight doesn't leave for a while and there is a bar around the corner."

I'm in a quandary and my mind waffles in argument with itself:

It's a free drink!

But he was in our space!

It's company for forty minutes.

I'm trying not to lead anyone on anymore.

It's a drink at an airport, how involved do you possibly think you guys can get?

I don't drink.

Get a water then.

Fuck my logical side. He must see my eyes come to the same conclusion as my brain because a certain smugness

71

enters his features. Imagine both our surprise when I open my mouth and speak from the heart instead.

"No, thanks. I actually am preparing for a really important job interview and I need to concentrate."

He looks stunned. I don't think anyone has ever turned this guy down before. I hope the novelty doesn't endear him to me even more. Some men like the chase. . . even if they don't understand the woman isn't running- she simply is not interested.

Take the hint.

But he surprises me by standing up and shuffling off. Not a backward glance, not a 'see ya later', nothing. Huh, maybe I ruffled his feathers more than I thought. I'm not too worried. There are plenty of women here willing to soothe his wounded male vanity. Besides, I actually do have an interview to prepare for and I'm going to nail it.

SATURN

I'm anxious and nervous. Foreign emotions that make me feel out of control. That's a dangerous thing- when I'm not in control. I walk quickly back to the Business Class Lounge and simply walk in, not bothering to show the attendant my boarding pass. Good-looks and confidence speak volumes. Once inside a private room, with no cameras, I let my features bleed to red. My blond hair lengthens and darkens and I allow my true form to the forefront.

I clench my fists to keep from raging.

How dare she.

How *fucking* dare she.

When I finally found the entity stalking my private moments, I traced her energy. Now I could locate her anywhere. I decided to confront her today, in this icy hellhole she calls home. It makes my namesake look appealing. I wore the mask of a carefree, sexy, beach-lover to speak to her. . . to understand her motives better.

And.

She.

Turned.

Me.

Away.

I growl in frustration, still recalling seeing her for the first time in physical form. As an entity, she had no substance, no figure. I merely could feel her very marked *feminine* energy. With each encounter, my connection to her grew stronger, until about a week ago, I could actually trace her location. I toyed with simply appearing in her living room, but I wanted more time to study her. So I decided upon getting to know her better. . . as someone else. The airport seemed like the most innocuous place to 'get a feel' for her, but she sidelined me by showing up first in the Business Class Lounge.

I was not prepared to see her.

I was not prepared for her.

I felt a tug inside my solar plexus as I rounded a corner. . . and there she was, in the flesh. Soft, white skin. Long, wavy, light brown hair. Large, guileless, green eyes. Slender and so damned breakable looking. I almost lost it then. So, the innocent act when she was an entity also translated into the physical realm, as well, huh? A decidedly new look and pastime for her. Sweet is not a side I have ever seen her wear before.

I decided to fuck with her and flashed a quick reflection of my true self before turning back around and leaving. I waited until she exited the lounge, listening to her

74

conversation with the attendant and then I watched, amused when she went running down the hall like someone was chasing her. At least she's entertaining in this form. Too bad I'm going to kill her. And I do want to murder her; to strangle her soft-looking neck for causing me to feel anything after all this time. The lust I can forgive. She always has incited a raging passion inside me, but the intrigue- this bloody piqued interest- I have not felt this since she was in her first, true form.

And it feels like a betrayal to my own self. A betrayal to the others. But I must pace myself. Today's venture has proven fruitless. She seems to be playing by a whole new set of rules and has changed the script of this drama called our lives. I have never- *never*- seen her turn down a man like she did to me today. Her ego has never allowed for it. Has she learned humility? I scoff. No, she has learned some contemporary tricks, is all. I must go prepare the others for this new mindfuck.

Her death cannot come soon enough.

CHAPTER 9

ZAHRA

As Mary promised, a car was waiting for me when my plane landed. A nice, nondescript looking man helped me with my bags and drove me to the hotel. Once settled into my room, I ordered a fruit platter and a sprouted salad. Fresh, *good* produce was hard to find in winter where I lived, so I was taking every advantage of being in the sun, wearing next to nothing (that was acceptable in public spaces), and eating a shit-ton of greens and juicy fruits while on this mini-vacay.

My flight here was smooth and unremarkable (exactly how I like my flights, thank you. I don't ever want to have to use those oxygen masks or my seat as a floaty because I have never paid attention to the flight attendants explaining how to use them. . . and I would be screwed), but I did find one thing odd: Mr. California never boarded the plane. I know this because I sat in first class (I freaking love Mary!) and saw everyone board. Maybe he got hung up at the bar with a new interest and missed his flight?

That sucks for him.

No woman is worth missing out on a connecting flight back to California if it means staying in northern Minnesota.

Pushing aside these thoughts, I now stretch my body over the queen-size bed, enjoying the sunshine that peeks through the curtain tops. I missed real sunshine- not the fake sunshine back home. (I don't mean fake as in 'not real', but merely 'not warm'. The sunshine back home is weak and merely alludes to warmth, except there never is any. Huge let down.) I order a light breakfast of more fruit (the pineapple was to die for last night!) and take a long, luxurious bubble bath.

There is something about a jacuzzi tub that makes me want to touch myself. (What did I say about judging me?) Besides, a marble, inlaid tub bigger than my bathroom at home, equipped with jets (hello, no hands!), screams to take your life to the next level: full-tilt hedonism. And I want to be really relaxed for my interview. When I get too nervous or stressed, I overthink, over rationalize, and over talk. I also get gassy. My stomach can't handle the butterflies.

TMI?

My apologies, I thought we were in the Trust Tree of Truth.

For once, I'm actually not wound from waking up. Usually, *he* taunts my dreams and I wake up an aroused mess. But I slept through the night. Maybe I was onto something when I thought my dreams might be an extension of my grief. . . maybe living in my parents' old house was not healthy at this time in my life. . . I guess I would see how the following nights are.

I get dressed. I agonized over what to wear to this interview. I finally decided to be casual. I mean, the hotel is looking for a *metaphysical specialist,* which does not scream overtly professional to me. I wear a deep teal shift dress, with an O-neckline, ending just above my knee. An Amazonite mala necklace and some strappy, flat, leather sandals finish my overall Bohemian look. I toyed with the idea of wearing pumps, but eventually negated the idea since I was likely to either break my neck or accidentally slip and stab someone with the heel. (I would never get a lawyer to believe it was an accident.) I wear light makeup and my hair falls in soft waves down to the middle of my back.

I grab my mom's briefcase and put in my interview papers. Hopefully, having this piece of my mom today will bring me good luck. I finish breakfast (the mangos are to die for, too!) and head to the lobby to wait for my ride. Although my interview is not until 10:00, Mary is having the driver pick me up at 9:00 to avoid potential downtown traffic and to meet with me first. The Arizona sun has only been up for a few hours, but it feels like midday already. I fucking love it. I was meant to be here. As the driver approaches the resort's corporate building in downtown Tucson, the cars start to pile up.

"Snowbirds." The driver grumbles.

Instead of putting it on the backburner to Google, I quickly look the word up on my phone. Snowbirds: northerners, mostly retirees, who come south for the winter. Hmm, maybe I should just look into retiring?

Oh, that's right, student loans, bills, no money. . . . well, it was a nice thought, though.

But apparently these snowbirds are causing the roads to fill up with cars. When we are only a couple of blocks from the building, I ask the driver for directions and simply get out and walk the rest of the way. Not only will it be quicker, but I would rather walk- to feel the sun's rays on my skin and smell the fresh air not laden with snow. I enter the ten-story building and follow Mary's instructions to take the elevator to the suite of offices on the tenth floor.

The doors ping open and I walk into a spacious reception area with little seating and a large, wooden, semi sphere desk to my left. Behind the desk is a polished woman, probably in her late sixties (I usually don't try to guess people's ages, since most get mine wrong. I got fourteen from the lady sitting in first class with me.

Fourteen. Good grief, I'm not even legal looking). She's wearing the traditional business pencil skirt, buttoned-down shirt, and lovely, red heels. I also bet she has never accidentally stabbed anyone while walking in them, either. She smiles when she sees me and walks over to greet me.

"You must be Zahra! Aren't you just lovely? I'm so glad you could come."

Her eyes are sincere and when she reaches me, it's for a hug. Her invasion of my personal space does not offend me like Mr. California's did and I relax into her with a surprised, little laugh. She pulls back, looking me over at arms' length.

"Yes, I think you're exactly what we need. I'll inform Mr. Al-Zahil you're here."

Mr. Al-Zahil? That sounded very *non*-Arizonian- but I was the *white* Zahra Delsol, so I had no room to talk. Mary walks behind the desk to say something into the phone and I look around. Behind her desk is a small door labeled 'Powder Room'. Another door near the powder room is for the stairs and exactly opposite the desk are two massive wooden doors adorned with intricate carvings. On either side of the elevator doors are two chairs, and I sink into one to wait.

"Is there only one office on this floor?" I ask Mary when she hangs up the phone.

"Yes, this is the Presidential Office. There is a conference room inside it though."

The Presidential Office?

Who am I meeting?

The head of the resort?

I know Mary is head of coordination, but to meet the Miraval Big Wig seems a little much. . . why isn't human resources handling this? I'm pulled from my musing when the phone rings again. Mary picks it up and makes a clucking sound of assessment before hanging up again.

"Alright, love, it seems they are ready for you early."

I gulp.

But I'm not ready.

Nerves rack my body for some reason. This morning's orgasm has done squat to calm me.

"May I use the restroom first, please?"

"Of course! When you're ready, just head on in. I have to nip in on the fourth floor to get something, but I'll be back up here. . . if you need anything."

I try to keep my face from falling. I was hoping Mary would come with me. Clearly, she's in my corner.

"Ok, thank you. I'll see you when I come out."

She squeezes my arm reassuringly before breezing out the stairwell door. Wasting no time, I enter the very lavish powder room. Clearing my mind, I bring my dreams to the obverse, seeing my red Monster Man fuck ungodly beautiful women, while I'm watching. . . and enjoying. And then I'm the woman and I'm not just an outsider anymore.

I'm a participant.

I feel every thrust, slow and teasing, to hard and fast. He tries to keep his hands off me but cannot help himself. His thumb brushes leisurely strokes across my clit, driving me insane. My own hands mimic his like in my fantasy. Discontent with the pace, I envision him speeding up, his fingers now a quick tempo against my slick center. Faster, faster, his hips keeping time with his hands. . .

So close.

I see him tip his head back and roar as he comes and I'm undone. Weightlessly I float, seemingly out of my body. Euphoria fills me and a calmness settles inside me. This is what I needed. To be so far gone in a state of pleasure, no other emotion can be felt.

Now I'm ready.

CHAPTER 10

ZAHRA

I straighten my dress and give myself a quick once over in the mirror. I look relaxed. . . if not a little sensuous. My eyes are slightly hooded. I briefly wash my hands, although I love the musky smell of my own sex, and splash a little cool water to my face.

There.

Now I look more awake and less freshly-fucked.

Squaring my shoulders, I march out of the powder room and to the gigantic wooden doors. Do I knock? No, Mr. Al-Zahil is waiting for me. I tug open the door. Damn thing weighs a ton! Trying to keep my briefcase strap over my shoulder, I grapple to keep the door open wide enough to slip in. I'm somewhat out of breath- I hope physical endurance or fitness aren't requirements for this job. . .

Inside the office is *enormous*.

Cavernous, even.

The left side is lined with pillars and seems to be a separate sitting area. In front of me stretches a rug, which leads to the back of the room. I would love to describe this place more, because it's an architect's dream, but my gaze is arrested by eight sets of eyes- all staring intently at me.

I repeat: eight.

And housing these eyeballs are some of the most magnificent examples of masculine beauty I have ever seen- bar none. They make the airport Surfer Dude look average. They even compete with figment-of-my-imagination Monster Man. The hormones still lingering inside me ignite into a forest fire.

So much for being relaxed.

To my left, seated on a bench (Which somehow still matches the upscale décor? Go figure.) are two identical males. Dark brown hair, glittering grey eyes, sculpted full lips. My insides give a squeeze. To their right, now going counter clockwise, is a man with the face of an angel. His eyes are like sparkling emeralds and his shoulder-length hair is so black, it appears bluish.

To his right sits a man with beautiful olive skin. His eyes are a warm and welcoming chocolate brown, as is his wavy, short hair. Devilry seems to dance in his eyes. To his right is a giant. I'm not joking. I think they used him to model the Jolly Green Giant. Except, instead of being the color of a string bean, he's tanned. His eyes are dark, his hair is dark, and he definitely hails from some island. He's like the Rock- only not bald and *bigger*. But everything about him speaks of peace. I feel calm looking upon him.

From Jolly's seat is a space and then a lime green divan seat for two. Sprawled wide (whilst sitting- an amazing feat) is yet another man. . .

This place is a total sausage fest- a hot sausage fest.

This guy reminds me of a jungle cat. His golden hair seems to change color as it catches the light from the floor-to-ceiling windows at the back of the room. His eyes are hazel and like his hair, they seem to shift color from second to second. Everything about him, including his proprietary gaze on me, screams *predatory*. I stifle a shiver and force myself not to step back.

What did the documentary say about jungle cats I watched last week?

Oh yeah, *don't look weak and never show your neck*. I quickly scrunch my shoulders up while trying to appear menacing (but still welcoming, so I can get the job).

I bet you can already guess how I look.

Wild Man is dressed like a cowboy that met Jeff Corwin. . . I actually think that just equals Crocodile

87

Dundee. Unnerved, I look past him to the table lining the side wall. It's filled with food and it all looks heavenly. At the end of the table, leisurely drinking something steaming from a mug, is another- you guessed it- gorgeous ass man. His skin is so dark, it almost blends in with his black business suit. His hair is equally shaded, sitting in tight coils against his scalp. His eyes are lighter than his skin and hair and are almost a buttery brown. His white teeth are blinding and off-set his skin perfectly. It's a wicked grin. This one is trouble.

And last but certainly not least, in the center of the windows at the back of the room, is a man seated at a massive desk. Like the others, he's large and inhumanly good-looking. The name plate on the desk reads 'Mr. Al-Zahil' and he definitely is not originally from Arizona. His skin is the dusky tan of the sands from the Middle East (where I assume he's from. . . cue the song *Arabian Nights* from Disney's *Aladdin*.). His hair is cropped, black, and precise.

In fact, everything about this man screams 'perfect'. His every feature is groomed to specific exactness. As is his desk. I raise a brow- I think someone has an OCD complex. (My father once had a colleague like this. . . I liked to go into his office and move things around when he was teaching. I'm a hoot, aren't I?) His eyes are deep, fathomless pools of liquid amber, surrounded by think, long lashes as lush as the hair atop his head.

(Another sidebar tangent: Why do men always get the best lashes?!

All they do is complain about them anyway!

End of rant.)

Mr. Al-Zahil has the look of wealth about him, as if he has never known a day of material suffering. Born with a silver spoon in his mouth and all that. I want to yank that spoon out of his mouth and replace it with my vagina.

Too vulgar?

It's just called *honesty*.

And you *honestly* would want the same damn thing.

Realizing that we have been staring at each other for longer than societally acceptable, I make my feet walk forward. It feels like forever to get across the large expanse of the room before I'm at his desk. He stands and I immediately wish I had worn the heels. Potential homicide be damned. He looks at me like he knows me.

It's . . . unsettling.

Trust me, if we knew each other, I wouldn't have forgotten him. The familiarity in his gaze morphs to something more like mild condescension. As if I'm not fit to kiss his shiny shoes. Pretending his apparent scorn does not affect me, I extend my arm out to shake his in greeting, like a normal, nice person would do. He begrudgingly accepts my proffered hand but stops mid-shake to sniff the air. His brows snap together in obvious anger and there seems to be a murderous rage brewing in his eyes.

Alarmed, I take a cautionary step back- but I swear to god, a chorus of groans and growls sounds behind me and I'm now out-and-out scared. What the fuck is wrong with these guys? Trying to figure out which evolutionary stance I need to take, fight or flight, Mr. Al-Zahil speaks.

"Your. . . perfume. . . is too strong, would you mind washing it off? We are sensitive to smells."

His speech is abrupt, clipped, and British, with a hint of something a little more exotic. Definitely was not expecting that, but I'm too baffled to bask in the deep, resonant beauty of his voice. Because firstly, I'm not wearing perfume and secondly, that doesn't even begin to explain their bizarre-ass reactions.

"Ah, sure, but I'm not wearing any perfume. . ." I trail off thinking.

I did just wash my hands and the soap was a flowery, girly concoction of some sort. Definitely of Mary's doing then. I raise my hands to my nose and inhale deeply. It doesn't smell overpowering to me. To my left, one of the twins makes a strangled sound.

"There is a bathroom through that door and some scent-free handwash inside." Mr. Al-Zahil tells me curtly.

Reminding myself I need this job, I barely give a nod of assent and march off to do his bidding. I have a bad feeling about this guy. Anyone who is that big of a dick within the first ninety seconds of meeting one another cannot bode well for me.

CHAPTER 11

SATURN

Even though I prepared the others for 'Zahra's' looks, they appear just as stunned at viewing her for the first time as I was. Seeing her (struggle to) walk through those doors, her soft, breakable form encased in flowing teal, her body positioned submissively, but her eyes raining defiant fire...

I could feel the others fight to maintain a façade of normalcy, too.

She seemed stunned to see the eight of us. No sign of recognition. I don't know what to do with her reactions....with her fake innocence. Her acting skills this reincarnation are superb. I'm not overly worried, though. Our skills have grown, too. She can only pretend indifference for so long. Eventually, Pluto will uncover the truth.

I look over at the others, assessing the situation. Some are like me, a vile mixture of lust and anger; while the others seem unsure. I had warned everyone to shut their senses down when she was near. The sight of her is enough to make us forget our mission... but the smell of her makes you think of the taste of her, which makes you think of touching her explicitly, and hearing her sounds of pleasure. . . Of course, I'm sure she planned it this way.

So I prepared us: No touching, no smelling, and absolutely no fucking tasting.

We cannot help but see and hear her, but we are to remain impervious. And I was, until she marched right up to my desk and shoved her hand out to shake in introduction. I hesitated briefly; she already thought I was rude, but I caught the look of challenge in her eyes. I would not lose to her again.

So I took her hand.

Soft, small, warm.

I broke the rule of no touching.

I could feel the others looking at me. I needed to be strong for them. Show them that *she* does not affect me anymore. I decided to take it a step further and test my self-discipline. This is who I'm at the core. I must have control. I took a small breath in, showing I could handle her scent.

It's delicate and feminine, and wholly her, but I caught something on an undercurrent. I growl in frustration thinking about it, my whole body going stiff. Because underneath her natural aroma was a hint of arousal. This time, I took a deeper inhale and it took all my control for me to keep my fangs at bay and for my body not to change.

She smelled of *completion*. . .

Like she had just fucking come seconds before entering this room.

The others inhaled, too- curious as to my reaction. I bet they fucking regretted it the second they did it, if their groans were any indication. For her part, 'Zahra' seems startled, even nervous about our reactions, not triumphant.

Did she really not plan to inundate us with her pheromones?

I demanded she go wash off her *perfume*, but it's really a moment for us to regain control. The scent of her orgasm has my dick harder than fucking stone. I know what she's doing. She's trying to break me. But I'm an iron wall of willpower. I'll not let this curse take us down. I'll break 'Zahra' first.

And when I do, I'm going to make her regret she was ever reincarnated.

Then I'm going to make her regret she was ever born.

ZAHRA

I come out of the conference room (which a small house could fit in) where the bathroom is. I walk around the table of food (and the hot guy) to stand back in front of the desk.

"Better?" I ask.

I try not to be snarky.

I need this job.

I need this job.

I attempt to keep the mantra in my mind's forefront. Mr. Al-Zahil does not even look at me when he nods.

Like I said: total dick.

"Allow me to introduce you to my partners. We are the Board of Trustees and the head of the resort. To my right are Mr. Uryn and Illu Blitznetsy."

Mr. Al-Zahil does not even point out who is who, so I'm left guessing which twin is Uryn and which is Illu. After my handshake with Total Dick you would think I would just

96

stay put, but my parents taught me better manners and social skills. So I stroll over to the twins, trying not to trip- because they are even more intense up-close.

"Nice to meet you. Who is Rin and who is Lou?"

I wait to offer a hand until I know who I'm greeting. The one on the left cracks a small grin. The one on the right doubles down on his glare.

Well, I know which one can take a joke.

"I'm *Illu*," says the one on the right.

His voice is gruff and thick with a Slavic accent. Damn him and his sexy ass voice. I'm so glad I do not wear underwear; they would never make it out of this interview. I hold out my hand to shake his.

"A pleasure, *Illu*." I make sure to emphasize his name like he did. "And a pleasure to meet you, too, Uryn."

I shake the other twin's hand. The one with a sense of humor. I turn to my left and introduce myself to the next man, not bothering to wait for Mr. Al-Zahil.

"I'm Zahra, nice to meet you."

"Arawn." Comes the brusque reply.

That's totaling three dicks now.

What a shame.

Arawn's voice is a thick, Irish brogue. His callused hand engulfs mine for a shake and I'm momentarily mesmerized by his vivid green eyes. I briefly wonder, on a scale of one-to-ten, how inappropriate it's to fantasize about blowing your potential bosses.

Like a six or a seven?

I could live with that level of misconduct and still be able to look at myself in the mirror.

To Arawn's left is the Devil. Not literally (I hope), but he looks like the proverbial bad boy. At least he's smiling at me.

"I'm Ermio Mercoledi, but please, you call me Mio."

Definitely Italian. His English does not sound as fluent as the others. Arawn and Illu look on with disapproval. Uryn's face is blank. I don't even want to guess what Mr. Al-Zahil's looks like. I shake Mio's hand happily. It does not take much to please me. Simple human compassion is good enough for me. Next to him is the giant. I hope he doesn't stand, like Mio did. I already have a complex.

"Hi, I'm Zahra. Please don't get up!" My request ends on a squeak.

"Why?" He asks in a deep, sonorous voice. It's as lovely as he's.

"Because I didn't bring my step stool to this interview." I smile, to show him I'm teasing. He chuckles and I relax. Everything about him is calming and reassuring.

"I'm Kane. It's nice to meet you, Zahra." The way he says my name makes my toes curl in my sandals.

"Spelled C-A-I-N?" I'm curious. It's the numerologist in me. The simplest of spelling changes in a name and it can alter your whole Destiny path. Kane looks a little surprised at my query.

"Ah no, K-A-N-E. It's actually pronounced 'KAH-NAY', but it's easier to just keep it at Kane."

"Kah-Nay, huh? It sounds a little like 'Kanye', so I can see why you would want to change that," I joke. "But I'm happy to call you by your real name. I mean, I get it. Most people call me 'Sarah', but I still want them to pronounce it right. Although it does get tiring correcting everyone." He shakes his head in sympathy. This guy gets it.

"I appreciate it, but I have been going by 'Kane' since I was a boy and only my people call me 'Kay-Nay'."

"Who, ah, are your people?" Kane gives me a kind grin. He really is a gentle giant.

"I'm from Kaneohe, Hawaii, but my ancestry is also Inuit and Tahitian."

"Wow, that is so-" Mr. Al-Zahil cuts me off by clearing his throat. If I were keeping a Being-A-Prick Tally, he would almost be at twenty points. Impressive. I give Kane a little wave and smile and walk over to Wild Man. I wonder if he'll be offended if I call him 'Mr. Dundee'. I peek at his face.

Yep, he would definitely get pissy.

His looks scream 'Jerk Alert' more than Mr. Al-Zahil's.

Four-to-three. That's the dick-to-nice guy ratio currently.

A little depressing.

"I'm Caedon Marx. My friends call me 'Caed'. You may call me Mr. Marx."

He has a low voice that rumbles out him and the slow, premediated movements of a lion. Also- he totally has an Australian accent! I had him pegged from the get-go, as well. (I had Mr. California pegged right, too, remember?

Fuck, I'm awesome.) So I'm going to chalk that up as a win, since *Mr. Marx's* introduction was clearly meant to put me in my place.

"I'm Zahra. My friends call me 'Zahra', but you can call me 'Ms. Delsol'."

His eyes contract and I suddenly feel like I'm baiting a tiger. A decidedly stupid thing to do, but he merely nods his head in a lazy, feline manner.

Moving along.

Last but not least is Mr. Mischief by the buffet table. Like Mio, he has a welcoming smile on his face. Also like Mio, he looks like trouble.

"I'm Nyambe Soley, but I would be most pleased if you called me 'Nyam'."

His voice comes out in a drawl, lilted with deep Southern accents and a hint of something imported from across the seas. It's as smooth as honey and so are his moves, as he catches my hand to press a kiss to the back of it. I try not to twitter like a nitwit. Pretending not to be affected by his kiss, I duck my head in greeting and slowly, laboriously make my way back to the desk where Mr. Al-Zahil stills sits, looking pissed.

"And I'm Khalid Al-Zahil. You may call me 'Khal'."

101

I'm surprised at this. . .

It almost seems like an overture of friendship- except he made it sound like a command.   *Mr. Al-Zahil* it's then.

Anything to ruffle Mr. OCD's feathers. I thin smile graces my lips. Just because I don't have a dick, doesn't mean I couldn't act like one. Khal (as I'm only going to call him in my head, because let's be honest, Mr. Al-Zahil is a freaking mouthful) immediately gets to business. He asks me to describe my services, how long I have been practicing, who I learned from, and the depth of my interests in the metaphysical sciences. I take care to answer him as thoroughly as possible, because I can tell this man loves a good attention to detail.

Me too.

It's the Virgo rising in me, I guess.

Khal and I might not like one another, but I'm determined to prove I'm an asset this company needs. He pauses every so often to jot something down on an open notebook, before refocusing his attention on me and barking more questions. Slowly, Khal begins focusing simply on my astrological talents. And so far, he seems. . . . *nominally* impressed with my skills. And I'm feeling. . . . *marginally* awesome, until he asks:

"Can you generate a chart by hand?"

I hope this is not a make it or break it answer.

"Um, no."

CHAPTER 12

ZAHRA

I see Khal's looks of haughty dissatisfaction. Screw him, I don't know *anyone* nowadays who can make a chart by hand. And trust me, I wouldn't be in this side-profession if I had to do that much math anyway. But I can see the restless displeasure written on the other's faces, too and I panic.

"But I can read a map!" I say this proudly.

There are varying degrees of confused and amused faces. . . sprinkled with looks like I'm an idiot. Fuck my brain-to-mouth filter. I hurry to rectify the situation.

"Most people nowadays rely too heavily on technology. Admittedly, I cannot generate a chart without it, but I do not use GPS to go somewhere. I use a good, old, regular map!"

"So, no GPS for you?" Nyam asks in idle amusement.

"Nope- well, except for that one time. I got lost because I was reading the map. . . uh, wrong, and I pulled up the directions to save time. . . and that other time. . . well, crap. . ." I trail off.

Navigation might not be my strongest point and a poor example of my skill set on my part. The guys do not look impressed. This in-person interview is not trending like the one over the phone. Well, maybe I'll end up being able to blow one of them. . . a nice one.

Not Kane.

He's too big. My mouth hurts just thinking about and I'm unsure if that saying about black men is true, so that leaves out Nyam.

So. . . hello Mio!

My inner musings are cut-off when the door opens and Mary comes bustling in. She shoots me a thousand-watt smile and asks Khal:

"Isn't she a marvelous thing?"

The question seems almost rhetorical in nature and Khal seems. . . cautious. . . to answer.

"Yes, she's *something.*"

He emphasizes the last word, but somehow phrases it politely enough to actually sound like a compliment. Mary beams at me. I beam back, almost giddy in my newfound knowledge: Mary is not just a receptionist. She means something to Khal and possibly to the others. Something important. And I'm going to use that to my advantage.

"Well, Mr. Al-Zahil was just asking me if I could generate a chart by hand. . . . unfortunately, that is not a skill I have worked to develop. . ." I trail off sadly.

Mary's smile turns upside down.

"I don't recall that being a requirement or even a preferred skill."

She shoots a look at Khal. I see his hand clutch the pen a little tighter. Careful, Mr. Al-Zahil, you're about to rupture your writing device. . . and potentially your spleen. Whoever Mary is, she's definitely more than the head coordinator. And she's on my side. Things are going my way again. Which is fantastic, but also concurrently disappointing because now I cannot blow anyone.

Shit, I have to get my head in the game.

Mary is talking about. . . I have no clue. . . because I'm too busy envisioning myself kneeling in front of Mio. . . FOCUS! Luckily, Mary is only highlighting the awesomeness that is me. I don't even think I need to work for this position anymore. She might just sell it for me. Bless her.

"You should come to the corporate picnic on Wednesday," Mary suddenly and enthusiastically invites me. "It ------------- themed."

She's bent over retrieving something she dropped from her folder and her voice muffles half the statement. I get down to help her pick it up, as the slip of paper has floated under the desk a bit.

"Yes, you should come get laid." adds Mio.

I'm halfway under the desk, retrieving the wayward paper when his comment computes. My body jerks in reaction to his words and I smack my head on the underside of the desk.

Mother of god!

That's going to leave a mark.

I crawl out, a little woozy. Kane bends down to help me up and sits me next to *Caed*. Like hell am I calling him Mr. Marx. . . in my head. Mary is wringing in her hands in worry.

"Are you alright, dear?"

"What. . . what did Mio say?" I'm a bit dazed. . . maybe I heard him wrong. Mio comes to stand before me.

"I said 'you should come get laid'. It's a Luau. Is that not how you say it?" He looks to Kane for confirmation, but I catch the humorous glint in his eyes.

He knows *exactly* what he said. He might actually be the devil in disguise. Now there is a throbbing ache between my legs, as well as my head. Mary studies me for a moment before announcing:

"I think that is enough for today. You're going to have one heck of a headache if you don't take some aspirin and have a rest. You can come back tomorrow and finish speaking with the boys then, I think. I'll just go call the town car to pick you up."

And with that, she sweeps out of the room, a general on a mission, leaving me alone again with potential demons (and a friendly giant). I look warily at Khal. Luckily, my head hurts too much for me to focus on how much of a douche canoe he has been. He stares back, sans sympathy. Finally, he leans forward and retrieves the piece of paper from under his desk.

When he rights himself, he gets up and walks around the desk until he's standing in front of me. . . actually, over me. (It's a little intimidating, but I'll never admit that out loud.) I unconsciously press further into the seat, but that only brings me closer to Caed. I suddenly feel

109

claustrophobic. Personal space, people- is it that hard of a concept? Khal's eyes glimmer with malicious humor. No, he gets the concept and gives a fuck. Clutching the back of my head, I glare at him.

He grins.

What a flipping mind game.

Exasperated with this entire 'interview' (which I'll forever henceforth refer to as *The Fiasco*), I get up to walk out. I need some aspirin, food, and a testosterone detox. I wonder if that is one of the resort's many spa amenities.

"Wait," Khal surprises me by grabbing my upper right arm to swing me around to face him. . . well, face his lower chest. . .

I'm definitely wearing heels if I ever have the misfortune of seeing this guy again.

"Here." He hands me the paper.

It's a sticky note with a list of dates, times, and places. I raise an eyebrow at him. And wince. Damn Mio and his bad English. Khal, of course, is unfazed.

"They are our birthdates. Come back tomorrow at 8:00; if you can accurately tell us whose chart is whose, then you have the job."

Is this asshat for real?

I'm an astrologist, *not* a freaking diviner.

A lot of people have this misconception, but I cannot tell you anything but my interpretation. . . astrology (for me) is about connecting to your deepest self for a more profound understanding of the mental and emotional catalysts that drive your psyche. Not for predicting the future or for reliving the past- although some branches of astrology do this. Arguably, a progressed chart, transits, solar returns, etc. could be used for this purpose, but again, I only use them on an individual level to aid in personal growth.

And like I mentioned earlier, everyone has every sign in their chart. While some features might be more predominant and scream [insert whoever's name], I really couldn't look at a chart and divine whose is whose from an hour's worth of interaction. I mean, Arawn literally only said one word to me- how the hell am I to 'know' what he's really like?

Whatever.

I need to leave before my head explodes. . . or worse, my mouth does. And my brain-to-boca filter seems to be malfunctioning.

"Of course, Mr. Al-Zahil," I say with as much saccharin sweetness as I can, "but there are only seven dates and times and there are eight of *you*."

I say 'you' like it's an offense. (That's because it's.)

Khal just looks back at me like I'm too much.

"The twins have the same date."

He says this like it's obvious. I'm not sure I school my features before flashing a 'get fucked' glance his way. I hate how he treats me like I'm incompetent.

"Of course the twins have the same birthdate," I snark, "But they wouldn't have the same time."

"They would if they were both taken from the womb via Cesarean at the same time." Khal snarls right back.

For a moment, he looks. . . stunned, like he can't believe he lost control, but he tersely turns on his heel and strides back to his desk. I don't even attempt to make eye contact with anyone else and leave before shit hits the alfresco painted ceiling (there is no fan).

Worst interview ever.

CHAPTER 13

MERCURY

I watch Zahra try not to stomp out of the room. I glance over at Saturn. He looks positively apoplectic. She always could get under his skin. Sunny is smirking. He and I are of a mind, being nearly conjunct all year long. Like me, Sunny sees something more in Zahra. As does Jupiter- but Mars, Pluto, and Neptune are too jaded. Like Saturn. Time will only tell what stance Uranus will take, but Sunny and I should be able to persuade him to our side. The rebel in him won't be able to resist.

"She's different this time." I state, no hint of difficulty coloring my English now.

"That is no reason to let our guard down-" Saturn starts, but I cut him off.

"I merely said she's different, not to welcome her with open arms, but even you must see this difference. . . Lina. . ."

I have a care when I say that name.

Once a reverent prayer on my lips, now an abominable curse.

I huff. "We have never seen Lina like this before, is all."

"Exactly," rejoins Saturn. "She's up to something."

"Why would Lina reincarnate herself in someone so. . ." Jupiter trails off, trying to find the right word.

"*Stupid?*" Saturn taunts.

"I was going to say young." Oh Jupiter, ever our peacekeeper.

"Maybe she thought we wouldn't suspect someone so stu- young." Sunny inserts.

"I don't think her memories completely reincarnated with her in this life."

I let that statement sink in. Saturn seems dumbfounded, like he didn't even contemplate this possibility. Probably didn't, everything is too black and white for him now. Too structured. I sigh. The curse is tightening down on him.

"Pluto, what do you think?"

I look to the stoic man on my left. Although he did not ask Zahra anything to get a specific read on her, he should have been able to see if her act was just that- an act. Pluto is slow to respond.

"I did not detect any hint of deception." He says this reluctantly.

114

Like Saturn, he hates Lina and wouldn't vouch for her to save his life.

Literally.

The others mull this around. Finally, Saturn speaks.

"We could use this to our advantage. . . assuming Pluto is not mistaken. Perhaps she'll unwittingly tell us how to break the curse."

"Or we could continue to search on our own and forget Lina." I interject.

Sunny and Jupiter nod their heads in agreement. Only us three seem ready to forgive and move on.

"No." Mars grates.

He's the worst of us, all but succumbing completely to the curse. Every day is a valiant effort to retain his humanity, his lighter side.

"We promised ourselves this reincarnation we would not waste our time. This *is* our last chance." He says this with bleak finality.

If we cannot get Lina to break the curse this time around, we will be forever lost to our darker urges. Destruction, delusion, rebellion, control, aggression, miscommunication, vanity, and Jupiter will exaggerate them all. . . until the world is nothing more than a playground of mistrust, lies, wars, and violence. And we are nothing but a plague upon our creation: Earth. Mars is right. This is our last chance. We must keep Lina close and use her forgetfulness to our advantage. . . hopefully she remembers something useful to us before it's too late.

ZAHRA

Alright, I have twenty hours to interpret seven charts (for *eight* men), find a decent pair of high heels, get a good night's sleep (that takes away at least twelve hours right there), and still find time to unwind from The Fiasco. Something has to go. . . .

Dammit, I need the sleep, I need to unwind, and I fucking have to do these charts.

Good-bye shoes. You were only going to hold me back anyway.

I drape a hand over my (still throbbing) head and lay back in my bed. I think a nap is in order. I can roll that into 'unwinding'. A quick nap, then down to work. I barely flutter my eyes shut before sleep takes me. When I open my eyes again, I'm back in the Presidential Office with the guys. Either my life sucks and I'm actually here again, or I'm having a nightmare. . . worse than those with Monster Man. I walk right up to Khal to demand to know what the hell is going on. . . when Caed gets up and walks right *through* me.

A nightmare, then.

And it would appear no one can see me.

"I say we fuck her. What can it hurt now?" Caed is saying.

"Until she cries rape. That definitely seems her style." Khal disregards the idea.

"Please, even you cannot be so *disillusioned* to think she didn't want us," sneers Illu.

"It does seem. . .unsavory. . . to take advantage of her apparent forgetfulness," inserts Kane.

They wanna screw some chick who has amnesia?

Wow- they need a lot of help.

Good thing they are rich; therapy is some expensive shit.

"Fuck her, and fuck her lost memories. She deserves a hell of a lot more than *unsavory*."

Caed looks positively savage when he says this. Jesus, what did this woman do to them? I would not want to be her. . .even to get a pity screw from them.

"Let Merc and Sunny deal with her. They will be able to charm something out of her, I'm sure," Uryn says in a detached manner.

"Or Jupiter can," Arawn adds.

"No," Khal states, "Jupiter cannot handle another private encounter with her, whether she remembers him or not."

Who the heck are Merc, Sunny, and Jupiter?

Code names.

Oh my god, these guys have to be mafia members or something. Rich, ethnically diverse, dangerous, commanding. It's all right there. Merc, Sunny, and Jupiter must be their lackeys. Not only are they criminals, but apparently sexual deviants. Well, at least Caed is.

"I think *Ermio* and *Nyambe* are our best bet. See if you two can get any information from her. Do. Not. Fuck. Her."

Khal puts a strange emphasis on Mio's and Nyam's names. Poor, amnesiac woman. She can't remember

118

anything and now can't even get a quick fuck from the devils incarnate. I don't know which circumstance is worse. I close my eyes and shake my head in pity. When I open them again, I'm in my bed back at the resort. I sit up and push my heavy hair out of my face.

Weirdest fucking lucid dream ever. . . and that is saying something considering my other ones.

I look over at the alarm clock: 2:00. I fire up my laptop and grab the sheet of paper with the boys' birth information. I open up my astrology software and pick a date at random. Plugging in the numbers and coordinates, I generate a natal chart in seconds. Hmmm, Aries Rising, with Mars in its exalted house and sign. . . squaring nearly everything. A lot of fire and too many cardinal signs on house cusps.

This screams *Mr. Marx.*

Next.

Taurus Rising conjunct Jupiter, strong Libra. Not a single challenging aspect, except to the moon. This chart speaks of someone earthy, grounded, pacifying. . .

Kane.

Next.

Capricorn Rising, Saturn conjunct the MC (that is the house of careers and public persona), this chart depicts a man in charge and who needs to be in charge.

Definitely Khal.

Next.

Scorpio Rising, conjunct Pluto, which is still in the 12th house barely, with the Sun in the 8th house and a lot of squares and oppositions.

Wow.

Someone who appears mysterious and exudes sexuality (that could be any of those guys) but is very deep inside. A catalyst for change. Brooding, reclusive. . . I get the impression of Arawn. I write his name by the date with a question mark.

The next chart is Leo Rising, with the sun just barely in its exalted house (the 5th), making a trine with the AC (that's the ascendant or first house). Someone full of warmth and life. A sunshiney person. . .

Hmmm, Mio or Nyam?

Nyam, I choose decisively.

Next.

120

Gemini Rising and all the planets are in pairs, conjunct with one another.

The twins.

And last but not least, an Aquarius Rising, with the sun and Mercury in the 3rd house. Mercury is retrograde, but in its exalted house. Someone glib, someone sociable. . . I sense a lot of trickster energy.

Definitely Mio.

I go back and erase the question mark next to Arawn's name. No one else fits that profile. Huh, I thought this was going to be a fucking nightmare. . . it's like I innately knew who belonged to each chart. Maybe I'm a diviner.

The time: 3:15.

Perfect, I'll get these printed and labeled down at the business center of the resort and then go catch some rays at the pool! Things are looking up.

CHAPTER 14

ZAHRA

Forty minutes later, I'm dressed in a monokini (which somehow manages to be even skimpier than if it were just a two-piece suit) and I'm strolling to the pool. The resort has *five.*

Five pools.

I would kill to have just one.

Anyway, I make my way around each, walking from one end of the resort to the next (it's quite expansive) and find that pool number four, the Grotto- as it's called, is empty. Perfecto. I set myself up so I'm directly in the sun's warm rays but my computer is in the shade. Things are still hard to see because it's so bright out here, but I deal with it. I have some research to do after this morning.

Firstly, I'm getting a new vibrator. Those epic assholes have me in a frenzy of lust (and a desire to do them bodily harm- an odd combination). A new, penis-shaped toy should fix me right up. I scroll up and down the page. . . one glittery model promises *twenty* speeds.

Twenty?

Seems a bit much. . . and dangerous. I want to get off, not have my clitoris *fall* off. I open a new tab. Next thing to Google: what do you call sex with eight men?

Oh, a gangbang.

Alright then.

I guess my interests have escalated to that level. Delightful. I try to type my specifications into the porno site I go to. . . nothing comes up for 'one girl gangbanged by eight supermodel men'. Damn. Moving along, maybe there is some raunchy erotica on Amazon to fulfil my perverted needs.

"What is a reverse harem?" An accented voice asks behind me. I swivel in horror. Mio is to my right and reading the screen over my shoulder.

"It's a story where there is one woman and multiple men. Usually three or more," comes a refined voice to my left. Nyam. Lovely. I wish the earth would open up and swallow me- and this damn computer. In my haste to stop them from reading more, I close the tab. (Because like an idiot, I forget I can just close my whole laptop!) This screen shows several clips of women getting railed by multiple men as brought up by my porno search.

"Ahhhhhh!" I cry. Delete tab! Delete tab! Could this get any worse?

"Twenty speeds? That is remarkable, yes?" Mio sounds impressed. . .

I forgot about that last tab.

Fuck. Me.

My mind finally comes to the logical conclusion it should have ten seconds ago: shut the fucking computer. I slam the screen down and hope I don't crack anything. Have you ever been in a situation so embarrassing you don't even know where to look?

I have.

When I was twelve, my well-intentioned mother bought me a training bra to open at my birthday party. My face looked like it was going to combust (I know, because my dad caught it on camera). One helpful parent of a friend pointed out that I had nothing to fill it with (the bra, that is). All the other parents chuckled. I wanted to die.

That is nothing compared to my embarrassment now.

A freaking cakewalk.

Worse than not knowing where to look, I don't know what to do. . . any helpful advice would be much appreciated. . . or have you stopped reading because you're so embarrassed for me? Thanks. I'll still count that as support.

"Yes, that is impressive, but it's overkill." Nyam's voice whispers into my left ear and causes me to shiver. I'm still staring straight ahead, not focusing on anything. I might be in shock. "Why do you need gadgets, *mon coeur*, do your fingers not work just fine?"

Ummmmm, what the fuck do I do? What do I say?! I shouldn't have shut my computer, I need to google this.

"Answer him, *carina*," Mio commands. Damn, these guys are bossy as hell. Fitting, since they are bosses, right? I crack myself up. (Don't mock my sad attempt at humor, I need a silver lining right now. . . and I'm struggling to find any. Even my Gran wouldn't be able to find one in this situation.) What was I supposed to be doing? Oh, yes, answering Nyam. As demanded by Mio.

"Uh well, yeah. . . my fingers work just fine, but they don't vibrate, so. . ." Not my most eloquent response, but at least I tried.

"Do you need help picking one out? Mio and I have keen eyes; we could help you." A keen eye for dildos? Now I have heard it all.

126

"No!" I quickly decline. "I was just looking. . . to replace my other one. . ."

"What happened to old one?" Mio asks.

"I donated it Goodwill," I blurt out. Motherfucker. I'm going to smack myself.

"Goodwill?" Mio queries.

"It's a donation center where people can give items they no longer want." Nyam supplies.

"That was, ah, very generous of you," Mio compliments me uncertainly. Yep, I'm a saint.

"It was an accident," I mumble. "I didn't mean to; I would never have gotten rid of Blue. My fingers are a dim substitute. They don't have enough stamina in them." I'm rambling because of my previous embarrassment. I need to stop before I say something in my new embarrassment. Sigh. . . too late. Honestly, I'm not convinced I have a malfunctioning brain-to-mouth filter anymore. I just don't think I have one.

At all.

Scary.

"*Blue?*" Mio asks the same time Nyam says, "Not enough stamina?"

So, I do what any grown woman would do in this moment: I run.

The Grotto is a pool, but like its namesake, it's surrounded by cavernous rocks, a perfect place to hide. Super mature of me, I know, but my sense of self-preservation is greater than my sense of self-respect. No knowing what I might have done or said if left in that situation. I scamper around some more rocks as quietly as possible. I don't think the boys were expecting me to run and just leave my stuff, so I have head start. I hunker down in the dark, drippy rock formation. Even with my eyes adjusting to the dimness, it's hard to see. If I don't move, they should never find me.

"Good idea, *mon coeur,* we needed to be somewhere more private for this conversation." I turn to see both guys wedged beside me. . . . how the holy fuck did they get here? I hope my terrified shriek conveys this message.

CHAPTER 15

ZAHRA

Well. . . . it must have conveyed something, because Mio sidles up behind me and slaps a hand over my mouth. His muscled chest is plastered to my back and he draws the rest of his body flush with mine. Nyam takes the front, until I'm sandwiched between them in what (I assume) must be crossing some ethical, work 'guidelines'. One of us should do something about this. . .

Not me though- clearly I have proven my maturity level in the last five minutes. I'm not equipped with one high enough to do anything.

"So, you must use a toy because you do not have the stamina to do it yourself, huh?" Nyam continues the conversation as if nothing has changed. "But I ask, why must you do it yourself at all? Why is someone else not doing this for you?" Excellent fucking question. *Why* isn't someone else doing this for me? Oh, that's right: no one can. So depressing.

"What you mean 'no one can'?" Mio asks.

Did I say that out loud?

I need a time-out, away from these minions of hell, before I tell them every embarrassing detail of my sex life.

"Well?" Mio demands. I shake my head. I'm not saying another word. Can't make me. Nyam gives me a very wicked smile. It says 'can, too'. My stomach flips. I think I just dared the devil and from the fire in his eyes, I think he accepted the challenge. My assumption is supported when he traces a long finger from the inside of my thigh to my sex. He teases me for a moment over the suit, before stealthily slipping two fingers inside.

"Breathe, *carina*," Mio rasps in my ear. I take in a shuddering breath as Nyam's finger brushes my clit and then circles the sensitive nub. I should stop them. . . close my legs. . . something! But someone else just had to remind me to breathe (which usually is an involuntary action), so I probably won't be doing anything. . . but moaning. Because I'm definitely doing that right now. It's like Nyam knows what I like: how much pressure to apply, the perfect speed. . . add to that him staring in my eyes goading me to look away, while Mio explores my body with his hands and mouth. . . and I'm a goner. Where was this all my life? Nyam smirks like he knows what I'm thinking.

"Like this, *mon coeur*?" It's posed as a question, but we both already know the answer.

And that is when it hits me: this *is* what I have been missing.

I have always fantasized about dominant men- which is my mom's fault for having those lame historical romance novels about when I was a kid. (You know, the ones with the woman half undressed in a ball gown, wrapped around some sexy, shirtless Highlander?) No thirteen year old wants to talk about *sex* with their parents, so I thought I could learn more by reading. . . I didn't realize that tripe wasn't an actual representation of reality. . . .imagine my shock my first time.

In the stories, the girl's first sexual encounter has some pain, but all is quickly whisked away in a world of sensational orgasms. . . In comparison, losing my virginity was a sad, painful fumbling. And every fuck after that was just a sad fumbling. I tried to pick men who seemed to take charge. Unfortunately, it never translated into the bedroom. So I chalked up my no-orgasm experience to teenage fantasy. That in the real world, communication was needed between two people to achieve completion. Except, *I* have never needed a guy to tell me how to get him off. I mean, they might tell me what they like, but I still could have got there without their input. . . were women *that* much different? So yeah, I kind of blamed myself and my predilections for never reaching the big O and just assumed men from my fantasy were not real.

I was wrong. Nyam is disapproving my theory with every stroke of his clever digit. He innately knows I need to be dominated because he has not stopped giving me mandates.

"Tip your head to the side so Mio can see me finger fuck your tight, little pussy."

Uh yes, sir!

And what's hotter than Nyam doing this to me? Mio watching. I like a little voyeurism. I like everything about this fucked up situation. I give a breathy moan when Nyam slips both fingers back inside my dripping center and starts fucking me fast. Mio runs his hands up and down my ribcage, before cupping my breasts and nipping my ear. His hot breath caresses me there as he whispers:

"We are going to make you see stars." His voice sounds off. It still is heavily accented, but the speech sounds more fluid. Nyam fingers curl inside of me and I forget my train of thought. "But first, you must be a good girl, and answer some questions for us."

I'm a good girl.

I'm a good girl.

132

Just please, don't stop.

"What?" Is all I can whimper out, sounding almost drunk. Both of them working me together is a complete onslaught of sensations and I can barely focus on anything except *feeling*.

"How do you fix an afflicted moon?" Mio croons in my ear. I don't respond. I think it's just his bad attempt at dirty talk. He needs some pointers from Nyam. "I said, how do you fix an afflicted moon?" This time the question is punctuated with a smack to my right butt cheek.

Ouch!

But the sting only fuels the fire building inside of me. Nyam is stroking faster and harder, while his other hand works my clit with an expert touch.

Almost there. . .

I. Am. Almost. Th-

"Answer Mio this instant." Nyam gruff timbre finally breaks the haze in my mind, but I'm too heartbroken to answer. I was so close. So damn close. I'm not proud to say this, but tears actually fill my eyes and I give a sad sniffle. Nyam tips my chin up and peers curiously at my face. Mio leans over, too and then looks at Nyam and it seems they have a silent conversation.

133

"Why are you crying, *mon coeur?*"

"I was so close. . . . someone else was finally going to make me. . ." I do not finish my sentence. I'm too upset.

"Is she being genuine?" Mio wonders to Nyam.

That's it!

"Are you two fucking *kidding* me?! You snoop over my shoulder at my private. . . stuff. . . follow me here, start sexy-timing me, don't let me finish and then accuse me of faking?! This is the only goddamn time I wasn't!" I hope no one has decided to use this pool while we have been fooling around in here, because by the time I'm done with my diatribe, I'm yelling quite loudly. The guys were not expecting me to blow up and both their brows are touching their hairline. Nyam is the first to recover.

"Will you tell us how to fix an afflicted moon?" *Astrology?* These asshats want to talk astrology?!

"Why didn't you just *ask* me that to begin with?!" I hiss at them. Both are looking at me like I'm some curious, strange, new creature they have never encountered.

"Uh. . ." Mio attempts.

"You're right. . . that was, ah, rude of us. We can talk shop afterwards." Afterwards? Were these idiots trying to

134

loosen my tongue over astrology? Using sex to get me to 'talk'? I feel like I should be insulted at some level, but I'm too damn confused and horny to even care.

"Fine. Whatever. Just finish what you started." I huff at Nyam. He lets out a chuckle.

"Okay, but don't get bossy; we're in charge here." And to illustrate his point, he pushes me back against the wet wall of sediment, pinning my arms above my head and smashes his gorgeously, sculpted lips over mine. His kiss is possessive and consuming. Nothing like his playful fingers. Intense. I love it and throw myself into it, kissing him back wholeheartedly. I forget about Mio, until I feel a breath at the junction between my legs. Mio is kneeling between Nyam and me, his face inches from my vagina.

Well, hello there.

He doesn't waste any time, shoving my suit to the side and sliding his tongue inside my aching pussy, almost in tandem with Nyam's tongue in my mouth. Both work together, building me back to the brink. Mio starts lashing my clit with his tongue and his fingers climb up my leg, until he has two curled in me, like Nyam did. I can feel the pressure building below and know my release is imminent. These fuckers better not cheat me again, so help them. But neither seems to be slowing down and within seconds, my lower body is engulfed in flames and my eyes actually cross.

Holy shit. . . those romance authors weren't lying.

Nyam gently lowers me to sit next to Mio, since my legs are jelly-filled and each movement sends little jolts of pleasure to my core. Everything feels deliciously warm and tingly.

So much better than my own hand.

So much better than Blue.

(Sorry, old friend. Sometimes the Trust Tree of Truth hurts.)

CHAPTER 16

ZAHRA

I take a breather on the cool ground to recover, but Mio crawls into my space and resumes kissing me. Both men use a lot of tongue, but do so impressively. They are not playing tonsil hockey. Rather, they are mimicking the intimate dance of sex inside my mouth.

Unhurried, exploratory, calculated.

I never thought I could come undone from a kiss, but they might prove me wrong. Mio's mouth tastes like mints and. . . me. I suck on his tongue, enjoying his groan and the flavor. Mmm-mmm. He pulls me toward him and I knock him backward to straddle his lap, while still consuming his lips.

New question: how inappropriate is it to fuck your boss, who just made you come on his mouth, in a pseudo-grotto open to the public?

Answer: He's technically not my boss.

Screw the rest of it; I want his magnificent feeling dick inside of me. *Now.* I begin tugging at the fly of his dress slacks. (Quick note: both guys are still wearing their business suits from earlier in the day. Weird, right? I'll ponder this oddity later.) I realize I need to get Mio's belt undone first, and begin working quickly to get to my prize, when hands trap mine.

"Another time, *carina*. We must talk now." The disappointment must be etched into my face, because he chuckles, "Promise." Nyam comes and pulls me off Mio, so he can get off the ground. Both their suits are looking rumpled and damp at this point. Nyam runs a finger down my nose and traces my lips gently, before placing a sweet kiss there.

"Now may we talk?" Sure. I'll just pretend it's not super odd they felt they needed to seduce me first. "Excellent, so, how do you fix an afflicted moon?" With my head clearer, my brain can actually compute the question. . . unfortunately, it doesn't really make any sense.

"What do you mean 'fix it'? If you have an 'afflicted moon', as you call it, then that is what you have. It was written in the stars at your time of birth. . . you can't change your natal chart." Both men seem intrigued by my answer.

"So we must change our natal chart then?" Mio asks Nyam. I scrunch my face up.

"What good would that do? Anyone can 'change' their natal chart by tweaking the time, date, or location, but it still wouldn't alter the inherent truths found in it. You're born when you're born when you're born," I tell them. Both ignore me while silently conversing. I try again. "What type of 'affliction' are we talking about? Square, opposition, quincunx. . .?"

"Squared. Always squared."

"Well, not every square is a trial. Venus square moon and Jupiter square moon are usually positive squares, unless severely challenged by another discordant aspect."

"Such as. . . ."

"Such as my chart, actually. My Venus squares my moon, a normally benign aspect, but my moon also squares my Pluto, Saturn, Neptune, and Mars- making it severely 'afflicted'. In fact, anyone reading my chart would only see harsh conflict via squares, oppositions, and challenging conjuncts. I do have some softer aspects, but the harder ones dominate my chart. And I *still* wouldn't call this a negative, though, because any hard aspect is generally balanced in some way through the chart. So, I guess the only real way to fix an 'affliction' is to find its balance."

"Find its balance, huh?"

"Yup. It's the best advice I can give. . . since you can't actually do anything to change your chart." Mio and Nyam grin. They seem inordinately thrilled by my answer.

"Thanks, *carina*. See you tomorrow, bright and early." Mio pecks a kiss to my cheek. Nyam leans in and does the same to the other side and then both just saunter off.

What. The. Fuck?

This job is way too stressful for me- and I haven't even been hired yet! I walk out of the grotto. I'm going back to my room, locking myself in and not thinking about anything until tomorrow morning. I shut my mind down, but a stray thought sneaks in first. . . when did Mio's English become so flawless?

SUN

"Well?" Saturn demands the minute we come back. Impatient bastard. Mercury looks to me, but doesn't say anything. It's a dangerous game we play, goading the monster inside the man. "Did she say anything?"

140

"Yes. She said a lot." I supply. Saturn throws his hands up in frustration and annoyance. Self-control is his bottom line and I see it as my personal mission to ensure he continually strives for it, not giving in to the curse. And I enjoy pissing him off.

"Did she say anything *useful?*" Pluto asks.

"Maybe," I reply slyly. Mars looks like he's about to sucker punch me and I glow bright, letting my true form through. He can try, but he'll get burned. Literally.

"Enough. We do not have time for this. What did she say?" Jupiter calls an end to our standoff.

"Well, initially, she said there was nothing we could do, except change our charts- which she feels is impossible or a futile waste of tinkering with numbers."

"It's impossible to her," Uranus counters.

"But not for us," adds Neptune.

"No, not for us, but irrelevant. No matter our reincarnation, our moon is always afflicted. Lina ensured this when she cursed us. No matter how many times we are reborn, we cannot change how she has patterned our stars." Saturn says. He's right, but I like to keep the idea as an option. There must be a loop hole somewhere in the cosmos.

"What else?" Pluto seems to have caught some of Saturn's impatience.

"She later added that every affliction is somehow balanced in the chart. To 'fix' the problem, we need to find and exploit this balance." The boys are silent, processing this new information.

"Balanced, how?" Jupiter queries. I shrug. I don't know any more than he does. Neptune starts chuckling.

"What's so funny?" Mercury asks.

"Let the little astrologist figure it out. That's what we are hiring her to do."

"And if this is all a front and she's playing us?" Mars throws out in challenge. Pluto looks insulted.

"I'm not mistaken. I did not detect deceit from her."

"We didn't before, either," Mars rejoins quietly. We silently reflect upon that betrayal.

"Let's see what she comes up with and then decide if it's truthful or even beneficial." Saturn settles the matter. Our self-appointed 'leader'. "Now, how did you two get the information from her?" I look to Mercury, his face a careful mask of blandness. I make mine shine with innocence.

"We asked her," I say. Saturn arches a brow. He does not believe me for a second.

"*How* did you ask her?"

"With my *mouth*," Mercury answers smugly. I struggle to keep my cocky grin under wraps. Saturn still looks uncertain, but he can see Mercury and I'll not be divulging anymore on the matter. Besides, we have new information to sort through before tomorrow's interview, part two. I look to Mercury and we silently agree- there is no need to point out that Zahra's afflicted moon is confirmation of her identity. Let everyone else just keep suspecting.

CHAPTER 17

ZAHRA

My silver lining for the day is I had another night of restful, dream-free sleep. It's only 6:45 in the morning, but I'm pretty sure that is about as gilded as my day will get, since the first half is going to be spent with those ass-clowns masquerading as gorgeous men (again, minus Kane).

Oh, but wait- I did totally get their charts sorted. . . so I guess there is that, also.

And I did have my first other-person orgasm yesterday- that's a positive, too, right?

Except I now have to see said other-person, plus his partner-in-crime. . . but it won't be awkward at all. Nope. We are all grown adults. My stomach sinks just thinking about it. Something is going to go terribly wrong, isn't it? Those fuckers are out for blood.

Mine.

I look at the ceiling in frustration. Maybe I should call in sick and just email over the documents to Mary? Then I could maybe do a phone interview with one of them later. Preferably Kane. Or I could cut all the testosterone out and just check-in with Mary. Solid plan.

145

Ooooooo, I could say I have my period.

Men are always squeamish about that time of the month. I smirk at the thought of their reactions. Then frown.

"You cannot be present due to a monthly, biological function of your body?" I practically can hear Mr. Al-Zahil's voice taunt me.

Ugh.

He's even a dick in my imagination.

Ok, new plan. I got food poisoning last night. I can't go to an interview if I have the turkey trots. (That's diarrhea, for all you city folk.) Love it. Time to execute it. I hear a knock on the door: breakfast is here.

You know- I lied. This is going to be a fantastic morning to a fantastic day. I set my cell on the table, ready to call Mary (she'll be sympathetic to "my plight") and open the door to get my food. A server in a crisp uniform is waiting with an impressive tray of fruit and some fresh-squeezed juice. Next to my food is what appears to be a portable hotel phone, some cutlery, and napkins. The uniformed man is cute, in a boyish way that will never turn me on again (damn those eight!), but a girl can still flirt, right? I offer him a big smile and a greeting.

"Good morning, miss. I hope you slept well. How are you doing today?"

"Fantastic! Thanks for asking! And yourself?" I say the last bit while seductively popping a grape in my mouth. If I can manage to chew it without choking, then I'll have achieved the desired effect I was going for.

"I'm well, thank you. Any plans for today?" *I think the grape worked. . .*

"Nope. I'll be in this room all day. . .so, you know. . ." I trail off suggestively and pop another grape into my mouth.

"*And how the hell do you plan to come to your interview if you're not leaving your room all day?*" Mr. Al-Zahil's voice grates from the phone on the cart.

I promptly start choking on the grape.

The server rushes around the cart and starts trying to do the Heimlich Maneuver on me. *Trying* being the key word. He's mostly just got a handful of boob and is pushing them up better than my bra. Finally, he lets my front go (thank god!) and gives my back a good slap. Good enough to send me sailing to the floor. The impact with the carpeted ground dislodges the (still whole) grape, which then rolls benignly three doors down the hall. I take a deep, shuddering breath and then greedily inhale more air.

Breathing: a seriously taken-for-granted activity.

"*The town car will be waiting for you in ten minutes. Get your ass down there and don't be late.*" Click. I gasp. That ass-rash (I made that one up. Say it. Fun, right?) can't talk to me that way!

"You can't talk to me that way," I say out loud, even though I know he's no longer on the line. "He can't talk to me that way," I bellow at the server.

The poor boy is already walking away with the cart and doesn't even look back. Why does that whole scene seem like a set-up? I stomp back inside my room and slam the door. (There's that stellar maturity level again.) I walk over to my phone and turn on the internet.

New thing to Google: do you have to pay bills if imprisoned for life? (I need to know this before I commit my first seven murders- I'm sparing Kane.)

I check the time. I better get going. I'm actually a little afraid to see what would happen if I *were* late. The town car is already outside when I walk out into the tepid sunshine, which is covered by clouds. If there is a god, he'll let there be a landslide of Snowbirds flooding downtown

Tucson so I'm hours late to my meeting. Oh, I forgot, *he's* on *Khal's* side. The ride turns out to be a breeze and I'm in front of the corporate building in record time. God is definitely on Khal's side.

If only I had a penis.

Then I could be a part of the club. Guys watch out for other guys. Women used to be that way, before the patriarchy turned us against one another. Now another vagina would not stop to help me, even if I were choking on a grape. Sad times, people, sad times. I make a mental note to help another vagina out today, *especially* if she's choking on a grape. (I'm still bitter about that whole situation, in case you didn't notice.)

I look at the glass front of the building, catching my reflection. I decided to be even more casual today and I'm wearing a pair of ombre leggings the color of a desert sunset and a teal tank top. I like teal- a lot. It's my power color. I'm wearing some feathered, crystal concoction around my neck and the same strappy sandals as before. My hair is in a messy bun and I'm working the grunge look. I might actually be trying to *not* get this job.

When I get to the tippy-top floor, Mary is nowhere to be seen. No weapons (a.k.a high heels) and no shield (a.k.a Mary). . . good thing I went to self-defense training in college. . . sort of. It was a twelve hour training divided into three Saturdays in a row. Four hours on a weekend day. . . well, let's just say, I made it the first ten minutes and decided I didn't need to know anymore. Their opening strategy was to teach us to throw our hands out and scream 'NO' at the tops of our lungs. I think the hope was that the attacker would see a self-assertive woman who would not be easy prey. . . However, I think we just appeared to be deranged, which works in our benefit because I don't think anyone would want to deal with that level of crazy. And I have been holding that card close to my chest for years now, ready to unleash the insanity at any given moment.

Beware.

Not you.

Potential attackers.

(Sorry, you know I ramble when nervous.) And I'm stupid-nervous right now, standing in front of the doors to the Presidential Office. I'm not even going to waste either of our time trying to give myself a pep talk. This is going to be brutal. (The Trust Tree of Truth is a sucky place to be ~~sometimes~~ all of the time.)

Ok, time to face the assholes.

I mean music.

CHAPTER 18

ZAHRA

I open the doors and (again) struggle to get inside. I
take two steps and hear a *riiiiiip.* My lace, flowy, power-
color tank top catches in the doors and has torn what feels
like half-way up my back. Anyone who wants to try and
give me a silver lining right now can fuck off. I'm going to
pretend this tank top has always been an open-back shirt,
but just because I can roll with the punches doesn't mean
I'm going to get all Pollyanna-ed. This is a sucky situation
that just turned suckier.

I can feel all eight sets of eyes boring into me, but I
hold my chin high and look over Khal's head, out the
windows. I'm going to survive this new fiasco by not making
eye contact with anyone in this room. . . except maybe Kane.
I walk until I'm standing next to the soft green divan and
wait for this debacle to begin.

"Sit down," Caed commands tersely.

I sit, as far left as possible, but it does me little good
because the Steve Irwin impersonator is taking up three-
fourths of the damn settee. I wait. Nothing. (I'm still not
looking at anyone.) Nyam moves in my peripheral and I cut

151

him a quick glance- but that A-hole is waiting. He smirks at me knowingly and winks.

Winks.

I cringe. . . does everyone know what happened yesterday?

But the others seem oblivious, save Mio. (At least, I think so, given my hurried assessment. Remember, no eye contact.) I tip my head back and study the mural on the ceiling. It's painted like the night sky with all twelve zodiac constellations interpreted into the background. One section depicts the moon phases, but it looks like someone defaced that part of the artwork.

Pity.

Someone clears their throat and I snap back to attention. In front of me are two denim-clad penises. Like a total professional, I shriek and fall off the divan. Luckily, it's a short drop, but I'm pretty sure when I get back home I'll not have an ounce of dignity left. The twins stare down at me, probably wondering what my problem is. . . neither of them move to help me back to my seat.

"Yes?" I try to ask politely.

I fail.

Uryn gives a small grin (that is how I know it's him) and gestures at my briefcase.

"We are ready to see your work." What, no reprimanding for this morning? Hot dog. I'll take it. I quickly snap the briefcase open and take out the files.

"Shall I give everyone their chart?" I query.

Illu raises a brow in challenge, but gives me a nod. I get up and hand out everyone's birth chart. The guys take a moment to read the dates.

"The lass got mine right." Comes Arawn's smooth brogue.

"And mine."

"And mine."

"And mine."

"And ours."

Until everyone in the room acknowledges how badass I'm. . . I'm not going to lie, it feels pretty awesome.

"Congratulations," commends Illu in a flat tone.

The way he says it almost hints like he knew I could do this. . . am I insulted or flattered? Whatever. I did it. That means I have the job. Which means now I can work,

153

set aside some money, look for *another job*, and still live here. Life makes sense again.

"Thanks. I'm an awesome astrologist like that. So let's talk business. Is there any way I could get an advance or maybe set-up a relocation budget to help me move? Also, I would like to review my benefits. Do I get dental. . . Wait, will I actually be an employee of Miraval or will I be subcontracted out? That affects how I do my taxes. If I'm self-employed, I need to save things, like donation receipts, for tax deductions, and other things li-"

"Donations, like those you give to the Goodwill?" Mio's English is sounding hacked again.

"Ah, yeah, exactly like that and I ne-"

"Zahra has very big heart. She's very generosa. Isn't that right, Nyam?"

"Mhmm, that she's. . . Zahra, didn't you give Goodwill your vibrator?"

Ohmyfuckinggod.

That's it.

I need those heels so I can ~~purposely~~ accidentally stake Nyam through the heart.

(Does that kill demons or just vampires? I could use a lesson from Monster Man, I bet as a potential vampire, he would know.) The office is shrouded in silence. Even the crickets are too mortified for me to make a sound.

"You gave your vibrator to a charity center?" Comes Caed's lazy, condescending drawl.

"Not on purpose," I huff. "I didn't know it was in the box. I thought it was just a bunch of random junk from my parents' house I was trying to clean. . . I knew I shouldn't have been trying to organize my personal stuff while decluttering. Or I should have double-checked the boxes. . . I don't even think I got a receipt for that donation. . ." I might be babbling.

Can you guess my embarrassment level?

"Maybe you should keep your thoughts to yourself. It would help you seem more *intelligent.*" Khal helpfully/unhelpfully suggests. I narrow my eyes in affront.

"Everyone's inner ramblings are dumb!" I defend.

"Yes, except you don't keep yours *inside.*"

What.

A.

Dick.

"Well, I'm not dumb, thank you very much. I have a freaking master's degree in engineering!"

(How suitably impressed are you right now?)

"Your resume said it was library information."

(Ok, how suitably impressed were you?)

I do some quick math in my head. So, it only took fifteen minutes for this meeting to completely unravel. . . that has to be a record of some sort.

"Can I just get my benefits package and go, please and thank you? I have some research I need to do."

To Google: available jobs in Tucson or even outside of the city. I want to limit my chances of running into these eight.

"Still looking for a replacement vibrator or a better wording for your gangbang search?" Nyam casually asks.

Why?!

Why is this happening to me?

Oh, no!

Karma is real and she's a total bitch. She also is in cahoots with Mrs. Gerty and this is my punishment for embarrassing that old bat all those times before.

I'm sorry, Mrs. Gerty!

I'm sorry, Lady Karma!

Please, please, please, I cannot take anymore humiliation.

"She looking because no one can. . . what are right words. . . make her vagina spasm in lust?" Mio half comments, half questions.

"*Orgasm* is the word you're looking for," Nyam supplies.

"Ah yes, thank you, my friend. She looking for toy because no one can make her vagina orgasm."

"I thought she was looking for the vibrator because her fingers didn't have the stamina?" Nyam evilly contributes.

"Ah, must be why she needs many men. So the fingers do not become tired. Good thinking, *carina*."

I'm concerned when I said I couldn't take anymore humiliation that Karma thought it was an invitation. . . or worse, a challenge.

You win, Karma, good freaking game!

Fuck it, I'm out of here.

I stand to make my way out of this personal hell (and here I always thought it was Minnesota in winter. Perspective, people, it can be life changing), but Khal demands that I sit down. Immediately. This guy has a serious complex. It's not healthy.

"Ms. Delsol, you will be working *for* Miraval as an interim employee. Upon a successful two-month evaluation and the completion of a project, you will be moved to full-time status and will receive a benefits package then. Unfortunately, there are no relocation funds, as you so quaintly put it, for this position. But you can stay at the hotel for two weeks while you find a new living arrangement."

He says this like he's bestowing the greatest of honors on me.

"I can't just move here for a two month trial!" I explode. "I have a whole other life in Minnesota. Either I need to come here or go back there, but I'm not bouncing back and forth!"

Khal is looking absently at his computer screen, drumming his fingers on the desk, and doesn't even look at me when he replies:

"Please, we both know you have nothing going on back in Minnesota." Well, I definitely *know* that, but he can only be guessing.

Well, two can play the bluff game.

"*Actually*, I have plenty of other options and I *do* have things going on back home. If that is the best you can offer me, then I'm going to have to walk. See, I spoke with Mary and honestly, it sounds like you guys need me more than I need you. *I'm the best you have!*"

"Don't delude yourself, Ms. Delsol," Khal's words rain down on me like a bucket of ice. "Just because you're the most competent applicant, doesn't mean you're the most competent astrologist. We could easily find better. It's only a question of time and money."

I hate him.

Truly loathe him.

He called my bluff and raised me a middle finger.

He's no longer invited to my gangbang fantasies.

Okay, so that's that. Time for me to just pack it up and go. While I have a tiny shred of dignity.

"What project?" I ask.

Fuck my mouth.

159

That. . . I can't think of an obscenely appropriate enough word. . . cuntmuffin?. . . yes, that cuntmuffin (a.k.a. my mouth) has gotten me in more trouble in the last forty-eight hours than any hare-brained scheme my mind has thought up. Is there any way to keep from talking? I think if you don't have a tongue. . . seems kind of extreme, but potentially doable given how my life has been trending lately.

"We want you to find the balance in all our charts," Illu says in his heavy accent.

"Specifically in regard to the moon," Arawn adds.

What is it with these guys and the moon?

"Fine and I have two months to do this?"

"Technically yes, but I want to see a report a week. To demonstrate your progress. And I'll tell you which charts to do when. Start with Mr. Marx's first." Khal commands.

"Fine, but I would like to see some paper work confirming everything we have talked about today." There is no way I'm not getting my temporary living arrangements in writing. Mr. Al-Zahil would totally renege just to fuck me even more.

160

"You want paper work confirming you need a new vibrator and a new porno search engine?" Nyam asks like he needs genuine clarification.

Shit, they are sort of technically my bosses now, so I can't flip him off or throw a stapler at him. I give him my dirtiest scowl before leaving. That pervert probably just took it as silent foreplay.

CHAPTER 19

JUPITER

We all watch Zahra leave and then Saturn, Mars, and Pluto all begin shouting at Mercury and Sun. I don't understand why. . . we all knew what we were asking when we sent them to get information from her. And besides, they upheld the 'request': no one laid with Zahra.

"What the fuck really happened between you two and Zahra?" Saturn demands hotly.

"None of your fucking business, *Turno*," Mio fires right back. Saturn stands, fists clenched at his side. Across from him, Mars rises, too, always prepared to spill blood. Sun sheds his humanity and nearly blinds us with his light. Pluto and Neptune stand in defense. Uranus does out of reflex. I stay seated.

I'm their neutrality.

I'm their harmony.

I'll not let their curses overtake them. I still fight for us and our brotherhood. But Pluto surprises me by blinking out sight. Mars and Saturn follow suit. Neptune hesitates.

"I'll go speak with them," he says, before disappearing, too.

163

Neptune is not usually one to intervene, but only he can work to change minds at a subconscious level. Uranus stays behind. It's hard being a twin and the planet of independence. One demands codependency from the womb and the other demands absolute freedom. Today, his individuality is winning. Mercury and Sun sidle up to him, bent on taking advantage of this, and subtly begin teasing him about the others. Both those two have a better handle on their curses, but the instigation and trickster tactics have amped up this last reincarnation of Lina's. I wish we could just have one day of peace, but even before the curse, we were a quarrelsome lot.

In truth, I have been keeping the peace between these seven since the cosmos birthed us. Usually, I'm quick to break up any potential dispute. . . before things become physical. Everyone is riding the razor-edge of their curse these days and I desperately try to be the final voice of reason. But today I listen to Mercury and Sun goad Uranus, interested to see what they are up to.

"I didn't realize Saturn told you what to do," I hear Sun taunt the blue Sky god.

"Afraid to have a taste of Zahra yourself? Afraid to see what *Saturn* might do?" Mercury sneers in near tandem. Those two should have been twins, but being conjunct for most of their life has brought about a similar relationship. For the life of me, I cannot figure out what they are up to. . .

"tastes like honey and her juices when she comes is the nectar." I miss the first part of Mercury's speech, but I have no problem catching on. They both paint a vivid picture of Zahra as she reaches her peak: how she tastes, what she feels like, the smell of her arousal. . . I can feel my cock stir in my pants. Just because I'm a peacekeeper does not mean I'm a saint. Far from it. My appetites may not be as overt or as strong as the others, but I still have them. And I want Zahra, regardless if she's Lina. Because right now, she's not. She's not the vindictive, possessive woman who tried to tear us apart. . . she's a lovely, innocent woman housing the soul of a monster.

A monster I once loved.

And I wouldn't touch Lina if she were the last woman on earth now, but I would gladly give up my immortality to taste Zahra. Zahra is the lightness to Lina's darkness. She's the balance Lina always lacked. That is why Saturn was so surprised by her physical form. Lina has never chosen to look so diminutive, so light, so weak. . .She wants you to know she's a force to be reckoned with, especially when her dark side comes to the fore. What Lina is up to this reincarnation, I shudder to think about. I hope Mars is not right and we are not walking right into her hand. I bring my attention back to the others when I see Uranus crash out of the room. I blink startled eyes at Mercury and Sun.

"What the hell just happened?" I ask.

"We appealed to his rebel side," Mercury states. I close my eyes, still not fully comprehending their tactics.

But one thing is for sure: this is going to be a fucking nightmare.

ZAHRA

I have an email when I get back to the room.

It's from Khal.

Should I accidentally-on-purpose delete it?

Too childish?

Well, this wasn't my year to improve my maturity, but I figure I better open it *or else.* No knowing what Khal might do if his precious email is not acknowledged. So here it's and I have taken the liberty to critique it first for your enjoyment. You're welcome!

Zahra (That's his greeting. . . At least it's not 'Ms. Delsol'.),

Upon speaking after your departure (Why is he so uppity sounding? Is it just the Brit in him? No offense, my British friends!), my fellow business associates (he means fellow douches) and I would like to amend your project. We would like a comparison of all seven charts in regard to our moon and how to find its balance.

Cordially (*Cordially?* Super British sounding word. And there is nothing *cordial* about this man.),

Khalid

Ugh, I want to write him back, so he can see what a proper *American* email looks like, but I have too much to say and spoken word will be quicker. . . time is money and all that. . . also, I'm super lazy.

(Remember: no judging. We are in this Trust Tree of Truth together, supporting one another in our weakest moments. And bless you, because you obviously have to do a lot of lifting for me. Thanks.)

I call Mary to see if she can patch me through. It rings for a bit and I wonder if she wasn't at the office at all today, but she picks up right before I hang up.

"Hi, Mary. It's Zahra."

"Hello, dear, I missed you this morning! Is your head feeling better?"

"Much, thanks. I think getting some aspirin into me asap really stemmed it."

"Excellent, what can I do for you?"

"Actually, I was wondering if you could patch me over to Mr. Al-Zahil. I got an email from him and it will just be more convenient to explain myself to him over the phone."

"Of course, but the boys are actually out of the office for the day. How about I give you Khal's personal cell number?"

Personal number?

I don't think Khal would like that very much.

"That sounds perfect," I all but purr, grinning evilly.

I can accidentally-on-purpose butt dial him at two in the morning.

(I accidentally-on-purpose do a lot of stuff. . . and you probably now think I have a problem with accepting responsibility. But you would be wrong. Rule number one to tough living: never incriminate yourself. Guilty until proven innocent, right? I didn't create the system, I just live in it.)

Punching in the ten digits, I wait for the phone to ring. . . except it doesn't. It plays music instead. A beautiful, haunting melody played by what sounds like a harp and violin. When he answers, I'm a little disappointed. I was enjoying the piece. And that small glimpse of non-prick Khal.

"Hello?" His sexy-as-fuck voice answers.

Damn, I forgot how hot he's when I'm not thinking about how much I want to tear his balls off and choke him with them.

"Hello?"

"Oh. . . hi Khal. . . it's Zahra. . . Delsol, from the office- your office?"

Best start to a phone conversation ever.

An exasperated sigh greets my stupid string of words. I kind of can't blame him for thinking I'm a little slow, but I still hate him for it. Wait, I actually do blame him. He and the other five have addled my brain; Mio and Nyam finished the job by scrambling it. Poor, poor brain.

"What do you want, Zahra?"

169

Whoops, I got to talking to myself. . .

"I read your email and there are some things I want to go over with you in regard to your request."

"And they are?"

He sounds less then enthused. I wonder if Mary is going to get an ass-chewing for giving me his number. I hope not.

"Well, a comparison chart in astrology is called a 'Synastry Chart'. This can only be done between the charts of two people. To compare seven charts will take a lot of work layering the wheels individually, in pairs, and rotating comparisons. The computer cannot do that. I have to. It's a lot of labor and a lot of time. If I were doing this 'project' on my own, I would probably charge around $500-$600."

I leave off there. We never did talk about money and what I would be getting paid in this interim period. Hopefully, I'm not selling myself short at that price.

"Understood. We can go over your provisional stipend tomorrow, but to make up for the amount of effort it will take to do these Synastry charts, I'll give you a house to live in, rent-free and utilities-free, for the two month trial. Deal?"

A house, instead of the hotel? And for two months? I can put up with him and the others for that, right?

"Sold, Mr. Al-Zahil!" I answer cheekily. "I'll get right on them."

I say a quick 'good-bye' and then hang up. I'll get right on them. . . but first, I'm taking a hike. This resort is situated on four hundred acres of land. The rugged terrain has been carved into riding lanes for horses and walking paths for people. Being out-of-season, the resort is relatively quiet and I could use some solitude to unwind.

I find a map in the center lobby marking all the trails and head off. The views here are stunning. Craggy, rock formations dot the expansive desert landscape. The sun reflects off the sand and it reminds me of the snow back home (but not nearly as depressing). It's so beautiful here. I could live here happily. I follow the map, visually marking certain landmarks sited on it, and simply enjoying the views.

At the two-mile mark, I spot a lesser-walked path veering off towards a secluded area. There is no indication of it on the map, but it seems well-traversed, so I decide to take a quick peek. After a quarter-mile, the thin path ends at a cliff dropping off into a shallow canyon and overlooking the northwest, where the sun is slowly descending in the sky. It's a spectacular sight. I sit near the cliff's edge, close enough to appreciate the drop, but far enough not to inadvertently fall off it. And boy, am I glad for that stroke of caution, because when a voice leans in to whisper in my ear and a hand brushes up my back, I nearly jump out of my skin.

"I did not mean to startle you, *kotyonok*." Uryn is hunched over me, grinning, and does not look particularly repentant.

"What are you doing here?" I ask in suspicion. My interlude with Mio and Nyam have me even less trusting of these eight then before.

"I was helping calm an unmanageable mare back at the corral. Illu and I personally train most of the horses for the resort's riding tours. I saw you taking off alone, without anything, and I followed to ensure your wellbeing."

I tip my head to the side, gauging his sincerity.

"I'm following the trails given on the resort's map. I assume Miraval wouldn't have open trails for guests to walk if they were not safe?" I raise a questioning eyebrow at him.

"Of course they are safe, but the resort recommends walking in pairs or groups, notifying the staff of your intentions, bringing supplies, and staying on the *marked* trails. You have no partner, no water, no phone and are on

172

an anonymous path. I could easily have my way with you and dispose of your body over the bluff. The perfect set-up for an accident."

Did this jerk just threaten to accidentally-on-purpose kill me?

That's my thing!

I narrow my eyes when he takes a menacing step towards me and I stumble backwards to a nearby boulder, looking for a weapon. My hand closes around a sharp rock. He can accidentally-on-purpose try to kill me, but I'm not going down without a fight. I paint my face in a fierce expression. . . it must not be overly menacing because Uryn just doubles over in laughter.

"You. . . should see. . . you face," Uryn can barely get the words out around his mirth. "Calm down, *kotyonok*, I was jesting. You Americans do not take jokes well." He takes another moment to laugh at my expense. Finally getting ahold of himself, he comments, "Put the rock down before you hurt yourself, or worse, that scorpion decides to fight you for his shelter."

I shoot a startled look to the boulder, where I grabbed the rock and sure enough, peeking from a crack in the stone is a small, black shadow. I let out a minute shriek and chuck the rock to the ground before all but leaping into Uryn's arms. He wraps strong arms around my body, hauling me up to him.

"I suppose I could still have my way with you. . ." He provocatively tapers off.

My heart is racing a mile a minute (from fear of scorpions, I swear) and I find myself leaning into his built frame (still, from fear of scorpions). Something flickers in his eyes before he starts lowering his head towards me. Then his lips are sealed over mine and all thought flies from my mind. His mouth is hot and insistent, claiming me with every sweep of his tongue. I compliantly offer myself over to him, pushing myself further into his arms. He gives a groan of approval and bends me further back to better angle his mouth over mine.

I genuinely don't even know how this has happened. It's like my hormones have hijacked my body and control all movement. A part of me disparages this unauthorized take over, but an even bigger part welcomes it. Abruptly, our kiss ends when someone shoves Uryn away from me. Feeling bereft, I turn to the intruder, hoping it's not a giant scorpion looking for a fight.

Nope.

It's just Illu.

But given the pissed off look on his face, I might prefer the scorpion.

He shouts something foreign to Uryn, who looks more than happy to throw down. I step out of the ring. More chatter, more posturing, and then both are charging each other like bulls. Their bodies collide heavily and I'm surprised the force does not drive them to the ground. There are no swinging fists, no punches, and no ear biting a là Mike Tyson. Not a single swipe. This brawl is all grappling, both men trying to pin the other down.

I keep a safe distance from the two- but also from any boulder, bush, or any other piece of scenery that could house a miniature monstrosity of nature. Their fighting style is fluid and both appear like they have done this hundreds of times. Is this typically how siblings settle disputes? Both Illu and Uryn are grunting and shouting more alien-sounding words to each other between breaths. What the hell are they arguing about, anyway?

As if they can hear my thoughts (and I didn't say anything out loud, for once!), they stop their movements to look at me. Illu says something in a different language that I have heard before, but cannot place. Uryn gives his reply. The air is charged as both men continue to stare at me. I'm

175

nonplussed by this mystifying exchange. . .I need a fucking guidebook for handling these eight confusing assholes and a special chapter on twin interaction. Maybe the resort giftshop has one handy. My mental tirade is cut short when the twins begin walking purposefully towards me.

The bottom of the canyon is starting to look more welcoming by the second.

CHAPTER 20

NEPTUNE

I attempt to calm a caustic Pluto, an oppressive Saturn, and a turbulent Mars. At my own risk. Being the cosmic empath leaves me vulnerable to absorbing their more volatile emotions. It explains my uncharacteristic moodiness these days. I take in most of the outer planet's eroded and raw feelings. With every passing day, I find myself more and more disenchanted with life. My twin tries to come up with innovative ways to engage my waning inspiration, but I find myself orbiting faster towards our curse. We are but shadows of our former selves. How pleased Lina must be to know she has brought us to our knees.

I speak with Pluto, Saturn, and Mars. My gift of altering the subconscious can only work if the person is open to change. These three are becoming harder and harder to reach as their mannerisms turn recalcitrant. Still, I attempt. These are my brothers and like Jupiter, I'll fight until the end to save us. I feel pride bloom inside me as they endeavor to open their minds and hearts to what I'm saying.

We must keep our hatred of Lina at bay while dealing with Zahra. If we drive Zahra away, we lose our chance at redemption.

As they relax into my suggestions, I feel a stirring in my loins. I quirk a brow. That is not my emotion I'm feeling.

Uranus.

Being the Gemini twins makes for an even more complex connection than we already have with the other planets. We are the intrinsic halves to a whole and what one experiences, so does the other. We are the celestial duality of the Milky Way. Uranus is the liberator and I'm the unifier. We are meant to bring universal stability. . . The potential for mass destruction when we are not in sync is immeasurable.

The potential for that when all of us are unaligned is apocalyptic.

I focus my attention on Uranus. Wherever he's, he's enjoying himself immensely, if my stiff cock is any indication. Odd, we usually share our women to gain mutual strength. If one of us starts something without the other, an invitation is mentally sent right away. When I reach out to Uranus, I find myself. . . blocked. . . which can only mean he's doing something he does not wish me to be privy to. Our sexual escapades have never been one-sided before and I ponder at this bizarre behavior. Why would he obstruct me, unless. . . he's with someone *illicit.*

178

Fuck.

He's with *Zahra*.

The truth hits me like a ton of bricks, but it's nothing compared to the desire sizzling through my veins. It courses like lava throughout my body, creating a fiery passion I did not generate. Whatever the hell those two are doing must be intense if I can still feel Uranus' emotions, even after he has blocked me. Time to go break up this disaster-in-the-making.

I wink out of space and time and open myself up to the cosmos, reaching for my fundamental link with Uranus to find his location. When I filter back into the third dimension, I'm standing on a ledge, overlooking the Arizonian landscape. In front of me, Uranus has Zahra locked in a fervid kiss that borders overzealous. It's as if he's consuming her, body and soul. Wasting no time, I walk over to the pair and shove Uranus off her pliant frame. In angry Russian, I shout:

"What the fuck? Must you constantly chase what has been forbade simply because of your unruly temperament and need to be aberrant? This isn't some *forbidden piece of fruit*- that woman *is* Lina! Whether she remembers it or not does not change the fact that she's. Control your fucking need to wet your dick in her two-faced cunt!"

His eyes flash something very dangerous.

"Don't speak about her like that!"

I'm floored. When did he become *her* champion?

He must see my bewilderment, because he clarifies, "Zahra, don't speak about Zahra that way."

Fucking Khristos.

"Are you dense?! They are not separate people! The current incarnation simply cannot remember. Get the fuck away from her, you stupid dumbass. This is the curse acting. You only want her *in rebellion.* Or is it because Merc and Sunny had her? Or are you taking a page from Mars' book and this is your sick 'fuck you' to Lina?"

I don't know why I provoke him, just anything to take his attention from being with her. My words have the intended affect because Uranus charges me across the short expanse of desert and then we are locked in battle.

"Fuck you, *bratik,* you're not my conscious or my keeper!"

"No- I'm you and you're not dragging us down to hell quicker via our curse because of *your* stupidity."

"If I'm you, than my stupidity is yours!" He snarls right back.

He gets me in a headlock and the air whooshes out of my lungs.

Son of a bitch.

I drive an elbow back until he releases me and then I circle back for more. Being of the same mind, we know each other's movements in advance. We will remain forever entwined in combat, unable to outdo the other.

"I breached Pluto's, Saturn's, and Mars' subconscious." I say conversationally, charging his middle to take him down.

"Really? What did you implant?"

He counters the move by throwing all his weight towards my center.

Fucker.

"To not drive Zahra away in their animosity. . . that we need her. But *only* as a means to an end."

Uranus seems thoughtful.

"Have you thought about using your gifts on her?" He asks.

I'm momentarily sidetracked by his question. Uranus uses it to his advantage and stomps down on my right foot. I growl in pain and ire. Use my gift. . . how?

"To release us from the spell," he answers my unspoken question.

CHAPTER 21

NEPTUNE

I think while maintaining a wary eye on my twin. Subconsciously suggest to Zahra to tell us how to break the curse?

"Seems dangerous. . . how do I get her to remember how to help us without her remembering everything else?"

Uranus shrugs.

"You're the mystic. You figure it out."

I glance at Zahra, watching us with wide-eyed apprehension.

"And how the fuck do I get her into such a state of malleability?"

We both stop tussling.

Fuck, I guess Uranus is going to get his little rebellion after all.

"I hope your seduction skills are as good as my mind-altering ones." I switch from Russian to our native tongue.

"Can there be any doubt?" Uranus replies.

No, there is no uncertainty. Lina barely could resist the two of us; Zahra is a goner. We walk to where is she's watching us warily. Smart girl. She knows we are up to something, but we don't give a chance to run. Uranus snags her arm and draws her back into his arms, his mouth picking up where he previously left off. I grab her hips with my hands and anchor her backside to my front. She arches into me, flaring her ass against my erection. Her hands are stroking Uranus' cock through his jeans, and my balls clench, feeling every caress.

I grind myself harder into her rear side and snake an arm to cup her pulsing pussy through her leggings. The thin material does little to hide her arousal and I press against her damp core. As she rocks against my hand, I nuzzle her neck and slant her head aside to better access her other erogenous zones. Nipping her ear, I whisper in my mother tongue:

"How do we break our curse? How do we become whole again? Remember and tell us, but nothing more."

She whimpers against Uranus' mouth.

"Yes, I'll tell you." Comes her breathless response.

I can tell she's already influenced by my planetary voodoo. I yank her leggings down, needing to take her mind to the next level and slip a finger into her drenched center. A guttural *yes* hisses out of her mouth, before she resumes kissing Uranus, her hands now stroking him harder and faster. I try to focus on my task and not the all-consuming pleasure I feel touching her and her touching my brother.

"Then tell me, *kotyonok*, tell me how to end this torture. What must we do to stop the darkness from taking over?"

She arcs her head back, a perfect picture of rapture reaching for her pleasure.

"Tell me," I whisper erotically. I work my finger into a frenzy, pulling her higher and higher towards ecstasy. Her hands match my pace. "Tell me!" I demand more urgently. I'm about to lose control.

"Equilibrium!" She gasps. "You must create symmetry between the dark and the light."

Her words end in a cry of pleasure as she comes.

"Fuck!" Uranus growls and we both follow Zahra to our own gratification.

All three of us breathe in heavy unison and collapse to the ground. Zahra shifts in my lap, unmindful to the wet spot marking my loss of control. Her mind is still vulnerable and open, if her contented sighs are any indication. I think back to her words. The darkness is our curse. We already knew this, our positive characteristics slowly whittling away. But how do we get back to the light? I murmur this question to post-orgasmic Zahra. What balances destruction, delusion, rebellion, control, aggression, miscommunication, ego and exaggeration?

"Love," Zahra mumbles in a sleepy voice.

"Love?" Uranus asks incredulously.

"Love conquers all." She says this on a dreamy sigh, before slipping into oblivion.

We both gaze down at the sleeping girl cradled in my lap. I almost laugh at her hippy bullshit.

Love?

Khristos, Lina really did a number this reincarnation. Uranus catches my thoughts.

"Why couldn't that be the answer?" He asks.

I roll my eyes.

"Must you *always* be so contrary?"

"Yes," he says with a dopey grin, reminding me of Zahra's expression.

Obviously, we need to get laid more. Sex is as necessary to us as breathing because it nourishes our immortality- but it also nurtures our shadow sides. We realized early on, each sexual encounter brought us closer to the zenith of our curses, so we worked out a system. Those of us with a better handle on our curses, or in need of reeling it in, would partake in *the sins of the flesh* and then share the power with the others. Only when we are all together can we manage to control our baser needs to feed properly. Feeling the power surge from this brief encounter with Zahra, we clearly need to do that again- and soon, as it has been too long since the last time. I did not realize how weak I had grown.

"Take Zahra back to her room. I have to clean up and tell the others what she said."

I pass the slumbering girl to my twin. He gathers her gently to his chest. She's such a petite thing in this body. I'm concerned about the extent that she produces these affectionate emotions inside of him.

"Don't forget to tuck her in and kiss her good-night," I say acerbically. "Lina will get a kick out of that when she remembers."

Uranus doesn't even bother to look at me as he disappears out of thin air. He knows I'm only ashamed about my own weaknesses.

CHAPTER 22

ZAHRA

I wake up late on Wednesday morning and get out of bed in a flurry. What time was I supposed to be at the office? I don't recall Khal giving me a time. . . I send a quick, apologetic text to him. Fuck, it's 10:45. How the hell did I sleep this late? I order a light breakfast and jump into the shower, leaving my ringtone on high to hear Khal's incoming text. . . or worse, call. My phone pings just as I'm finishing up and I slide open the glass doors to get it.

We do not need you at the office today. Start working on those charts. Mary will contact you about your return flight, housing, and finances.

I let out a relieved breath. God, that could have been a disaster. I crack my neck and rub it to get out the kinks. My mind still feels heavy from sleep, the shower doing little to awaken me. Why am I so drowsy? What time did I go to bed? I try to recall last night's events, but nothing comes to mind. Just blankness- no memories, no dreams. That makes day three of no nighttime visions. . . I actually kind of miss them a little. . . I mean, is it super fucked up to like to be dream-screwed by a monster while inside another woman's body?

Don't answer that.

I shuffle over to the table and open my laptop to get to work. I stifle a yawn. So sleepy. I hear a noise outside my door and go to open it, thinking my breakfast is here. Instead, a man in what looks like a hazard suit's outside spraying something along the floor boards. Um, is it safe for those of us not in hazmat gear to be around whatever this guy is spraying? I don't need my braincells scrambled any more than they have been this trip, thank you very much. I shut the door and call down to the front desk, expressing my concern.

"Of course, ma'am," the concierge assures me. "Those workers are required by law to wear those uniforms, but the poison is not toxic to humans."

I snort.

How likely is a poison *not toxic* to everything and everyone?

The lady is still rambling on, "We spray quarterly to mitigate insects, spiders, scorpions, and other creepy crawlers from being on the property."

I shudder. Gross, no bugs for me. And scorpions?

Hell no.

I hang up the phone and go back to my computer. A sudden flash of me standing near a rock-strewn precipice looking at a small, but terrifying black shadow with a poison-barbed tail flits across my mind.

What the fuck was that?

My breathing has sped up and I unexpectedly feel anxious. I need some food in me. I push aside my discomfort and pull up Caed's chart. *Yeesh.* And I thought my wheel had some hard aspects. This guy is walking time-bomb of volatility. The guys just want me to look at their moons, but astrology does not work that way. Their moon is only a small sliver of the overall picture and to find an anecdote to their 'affliction', the entire chart must be read and analyzed.

Fuck, this is going to take forever.

I see where the moon is placed, what aspects it, what houses and signs the aspected planets are in. . . There's a lot of masculine energy in Caed's chart, with fire and air being the dominant elements. Aries and Gemini are on the first and second angular house cusps. . . Looking at the glyph symbolizing the stellar twins , my mind drifts to Uryn and Illu.

An image of us locked in carnal delight flares to life in my mind's eye.

The scene feels like a hazy dream I'm trying to remember, but my body reacts all the same. I relax, trying not to force anything, and more phantasmagorias come flooding in. Uryn kissing me ardently, Illu touching me explicitly, me rubbing Uryn through his pants. . . us all coming. . . I'm worked up, both mentally and physically.

Where the hell did these. . . *mental pictures*. . . come from?

Not only do I not recall fantasizing about them individually or as a pair, but my imaginings have never been that *vivid*. It's official: those eight might literally be driving me past the brink of insanity. I need a break. I grab my sandals from the floor and plop down to put them on. As I'm tying the strap, some dust and pebbles fall off the bottom onto the floor. My heart freezes. . . I went for a walk yesterday. A hike through one of the resort's trails. . . where I later took an unmarked path. . .

And Uryn showed up.

Then Illu.

Then shit hit the atmospheric barrier (because there is no fan in the sky) before raining back down on me. Because those visions were not *dreams*, but actual memories.

What the fuck, what the fuck, what the fuck!

I have a mini freak out. How did I get back to my hotel room? What happened after our inappropriate grope-fest? Why couldn't I remember everything?

WAIT!

Did those dickbags drug me?!

Suddenly, I'm a ball of rage.

How dare they?

How fucking dare they?!

They took *advantage* of me.

I did not give them consent to touch me. (And let's not quibble over the fact that I would probably always welcome their hands on me, regardless of the situation. That's *not* the point right now. Let's circle back to them touching me without *my* permission- *that's* the point.)

Well, hell hath no fury like a woman scorned. . . also, a woman taken advantage of and potentially drugged.

Those bastards were going to get a taste of my medicine. I would sue them for sexual assault (if I could find a lawyer willing to believe I didn't truly want those two touching me. . .), take their millions, and set myself up on a private island! I'm storming about my room, when I suddenly recall Illu's strange questions. The whole scenario seems like a déjà vu of my time with Mio and Nyam. . . and a chill runs down my spine.

What the fuck was really going on?

They were hiding something and using me to get the answers. Well, fuck them. *Now* I was going to get some answers. I slip out of my room and downstairs, until I'm outside the main entrance. A taxi is just dropping off a couple and I quickly get in before he can drive away.

"Downtown, please, to the Miraval Corporate Building."

I give him an approximation of the address and settle back, letting myself work into a fit of temper.

Those cocksuckers are going to rue the day they messed with Zahra Delsol!

When the taxi pulls in front of the reflective edifice, I throw some money at the cab driver and jump out, slamming the door. I let my anger simmer just under the surface, careful not to unleash it on some poor passerby. Although, in retrospect, I'm sure this place is jam-packed with disgruntled employees who want to tell the company heads where they can shove it.

I should lead a coup. Unfortunately, I'm on a personal quest for justice.

And vengeance.

Those two go together, right?

I'll just graciously start the revolution and the discontented souls of this establishment could follow in my footsteps afterwards.

You're welcome, fellow employees.

CHAPTER 23

ZAHRA

I tap my foot impatiently in the elevator. When the doors open, I march out. Again, Mary is not at the desk. A good thing. I would hate to have to alienate her, in case she chose the boys over me. I whip open the big, oak door. My anger gives me strength and it silently swings ajar. With that, I burst into the room, hellbent on a mission for some answers. I take two steps inside and skid to a stop. My eyes widen and my mind blanks. . .

What the fuck am I even looking at?

Words actually fail to describe this indecent scene. . . let's just say the spectacle before me would make the dirtiest hooker blush.

Two girls are draped over the twins' laps, kissing and fondling each other's breasts; another girl is sucking Arawn's dick like it's a lollipop. Kane and Mio are simply taking in the erotic tableau, while Nyam is stroking himself through his dress slacks. To finish this inappropriate office scene, Caed has a girl spread eagle over Khal's desk, and is licking her pussy like a cat with a bowl of cream, while Khal is holding the girl's arms above her head and watching the entire thing. I make sure I have an appropriately appalled

197

look on my face, but in truth, I'm equal parts turned on and jealous.

Lucky skanks.

Before I can even formulate a plan of action- I mean, seriously, what the fuck does someone say to this level of debauchery, Khal shifts and his unbuttoned dress shirt parts. A tattoo comes into focus.

It's a sickle.

Right above his left pectoral.

I suck in a horrified breath, which somehow, he hears across the room and over the revelry.

Do vampires have super hearing?

Our eyes lock, mine widen in shock, his narrow in something more sinister and I do the only logical thing:

I scream.

A bloodcurdling, ear-piercing, window-shattering scream.

I mean, what would you do if the monster from your dreams was *real?*

Of course, this gets an immediate reaction and all sexual activity comes to a halt. I'm like a screaming cock block. My terrified wail has not even begun to taper off, and to my surprise, the other girls in the room start joining in. . . . are they screaming because they know they are in a room full of monsters, too?

Huh, well, I scream, you scream, we all scream because we are going to get killed by vampires!

The guys honestly don't look like they are going to kill us. . . well, Khal does, but the rest just seem a little confused. I let my scream die down. Slowly, the other girls quiet down, too.

"Why are you guys- ah, I mean, girls screaming?" The one in front of Arawn peers over from between his legs and says, "We thought you saw a mouse."

As if this were an obvious thing.

How the hell does she know that is what the other girls are screaming about?

But the other three are nodding emphatically in agreement.

Now I'm confused.

Are these women stupid?

How *dare* Khal insinuate my lack of competency when he has a gaggle of leg-spreading morons at his beck and call!

The proverbial light bulb blinks on above my head and I get an evil idea.

"There is!" I shout, pointing towards where Mr. Al-Zahil the Verified Vampire is standing. "It just scurried under the desk. Oh, there it goes!"

And I start screeching like a maniac again.

This gets an immediate (and expected) reaction:

The girls lose their shit and start screaming, while now running around like chickens with their heads cut off.

"Watch out! You almost stepped on it!" I'm adding fuel to this hilarious fire.

The four girls, in varying levels of disarray, run in circles still yelling, and then make a stampede toward the door. I quickly jump to the side as they crash out as one and slam the door shut behind them, hopefully locking the 'mouse' inside. I let out a little chuckle.

What gullible little fools.

I turn back and realize I'm alone in a room of monsters.

Khal is right. I'm an idiot.

So, again, I do the only logic thing (which is not scream this time, because I'm certain Mr. Al-Zahil *will* strangle me):

I get defensive.

And mouthy.

A wonderful combination to pacify angry monsters.

"I knew you were a vampire!" I shout, jabbing a finger towards Khal.

I feel ever so vindicated in this moment, but I'm sure I'll later question my reasoning in goading someone who drinks human blood for sustenance.

"I'm not a vampire," comes his cool and irritated response.

Gasp! He's already trying to use his mind powers on me, but I'll not be swayed! I assess my mental state for any indication of mind control taking hold. . . nope, his unnatural influences do not work on me!

"Ha!" I crow. "Your vampire mind controlling powers have no sway over me!

He looks at me like I'm a bulb short of a fuse.

"Vampires do not have mind control powers."

"So, you *admit* you're a vampire!"

He raises an eyebrow, but it comes across as an eye roll.

"Vampires don't have mind control powers because there *are* no such things as vampires. And since there are no such thing as vampires, then I clearly cannot be one."

How dare he sound so reasonable!

"Well, I *do* know you're a dick," I mumble under my breath.

"Excuse me?"

Shit, I forgot about his not-vampire, super ability to hear. Maybe I should pretend I see another mouse and make a break for it? Probably one of my better ideas. I take a step back and pivot on my heel. I keep my head turned towards the guys as I run for my escape and slam headlong into Arawn. I crane my head back, confused.

He was just sitting down!

Oh. . . these non-vampires also have super speed.

Afraid I might do something even dumber, like piss myself, I allow the dark fog of unconsciousness to take me under.

"You're not real, just a figment of my subconscious, overactive mind. This is just a dream again."

Barely hanging on, I weakly tack on some threats, too, just in case.

"Don't eat me. I taste terrible. And I'll come back and haunt you. I'll break up your every orgy."

Then I faint away.

"You already haunt us," is the echoing retort.

CHAPTER 24

MARS

I look down at the unconscious girl Pluto passed to me. It seems Zahra's past is catching up with her. Saturn is pissed. He never planned to let the little wraith know our true identities. Initially, he lured her here to *finish* her, but only after getting those crucial answers first, of course. But when we learned of her apparent forgetfulness, we agreed to work it to our advantage. The most important thing was to use her knowledge to help us without her remembering Lina. Paramount to this was not letting her know about the real men we housed inside these human bodies.

She stirs in my arms.

This should be interesting.

When her eyelashes flutter open, I expect fear and panic to envelope her. To her credit, she did just learn monsters were real. What I do not expect is the blazing indignation swirling in the depths of her glass-green eyes. She sits up in my lap, glaring at me, before snapping:

"If you fuckers took advantage of me *again*, so help m-"

"We didn't make you touch us, *little girl*."

205

I effectively cut off her invective. I swear some steam leaks out of her ears. I try to hold my grin in check. I never know what she's going to do next and damned if I don't actually admire her spunk a bit.

"*Little girl?*" She all but spews the word like it's a filthy epithet.

"Yes. Are you not *little* and a *girl?*" I cock my head to the side, like I'm truly questioning her words, adding patronizing stress to my logic. Zahra hates when we intimate that she's dimwitted.

"Of course," she says smoothly. "But I can't *want* something I'm not *cognizant* for, now can I, *dickhead?*"

I blink. What did she just call me?

She smiles obnoxiously.

"Do you not have a *dick* and a *head?*" She asks in mock innocence.

Everyone holds their breath, waiting for the predictable explosion. . .

Instead, I tip my head back and laugh. Fuck. This girl, she's an unforeseen firebrand. I look down on her upturned face, seeing the irritation roll across her features at my reaction. She lets out a grumble before shoving off

206

me. . . and falling to the floor. I don't waste my time trying to help her. She doesn't want it anyway.

"Well then, just let me make myself perfectly clear: If one of you whoremongering bastards touches me one more damn time without my permission, I'm going to cut off your dicks, slap a choking hazard on it, and shove 'em down your fucking throats!"

Bloodthirsty, little vixen. I definitely can see the Lina in her now.

"Did she just call our dicks tiny?" Sunny laughs. He finds her even more amusing than me.

Zahra throws her hands up in exasperation. She's tangoing with eight men who are gods trapped in human bodies- we have some complexes. Complexes of her doing, so she can deal with it. I frown, thinking of our human forms. Part of Lina's curse was to demasculinize our pride by placing us in a weaker, human shell. This also ensured we would continually experience an afflicted moon with every earthly reincarnation.

Our true forms could come out on occasion, if we have fed, and only for short bursts of time. We have not been at our full strength in nearly 4,000 years. I miss the Hellenistic era.

I look at Zahra: *sweet, clueless Zahra.*

The key to our freedom.

Unfortunately, that probably means we are going to have to break her.

A shame.

Her shell this reincarnation will just have to be a casualty of *war.* I smile at my pun.

Yes, it's time.

We are finally going to reclaim our godhood.

ZAHRA

So, I would like to take a moment to recap the absurdity that is my life. Firstly, the monster (who apparently is not a vampire) from my dreams is real. And he has seven other asshole, monster friends. Secondly, they are my bosses.

End of recap. I think those two bullet points say enough.

Waking up in Caed's lap was also not a highlight of my day. Ok, maybe it was, a little. . .

Until he spoke.

Cripes, why couldn't that sting ray have barbed his heart instead of Steve Irwin's? It would have done the world a real favor. Except, I'm not convinced Caed has a heart. . . or can even die. . . so it's just wishful thinking on my part. A girl's gotta dream though, right? I realize the dickwads are talking about me and tune-in to their words. Khal is simply *astounded* that I didn't figure this out sooner. . .

I need to figure out how to off these epic douches. But first, I need to defend myself. Looking at Khal, I say:

"Stop treating me like I'm an imbecile, how was I supposed to put two and two together to get eight?"

(FYI: I'm being facetious. I know it equals four, in case you think I'm an airhead, too.)

"I mean, come on! You have cropped hair, tanned, normal, *human* skin, not-red eyes, no fangs, and a freaking British accent!"

He rolls his eyes without ever moving them. It's kind of unnerving (and secretly impressive) how easily he can express his disdain without even twitching a muscle.

"That is because I used the language of the gods in 'your dreams'."

He actually makes finger quotes. How far *is* that stick shoved up his ass? Then I focus on his words. Huh. . . I understood the language of the gods?

Wow.

Does this make me one, then?

I'm quick to point out my awesome logic.

"Slaves need to know the language, too- to do their master's bidding." Khal drawls.

Did this fucker just call me an indentured servant? Swear to god, I'm goin- Wait, wait, wait, wait. . . *language of the gods*. . . No.

No. No. No. No.

These eight were *gods*?!

"Nope. I don't believe it. No way you jackasses are gods." I cross my arms and nod my head for good measure.

Khal raises a brow before effortlessly shifting into the hulking red-skinned beast from my dreams. When scary shit happens in your dreams, it feels like real life. Oddly enough, when scary shit happens in real life, it all too often feels surreal. Like now, as I take in the rubicund man before me. . . my mind does not even try to process the scene. It jumped ship a long time ago and I'm operating on pure instinct.

And instinct is telling me to protect myself.

I walk over to the table of food and pick up a silver-plated platter of cheeses, which I unceremoniously dump in the vacated spot on the table. I then start refilling the platter with generous heaps of mouthwatering linguini in a creamy, aromatic sauce. I can feel the guys' eyes watching me. I pick up the platter, making sure it's not too heavy for me to handle, and walk towards Khal, who is towering over his desk. When I'm about three feet away, I stop, look him in the eye, and fling the platter back like a catapult, before launching the food at his face.

Nobody moves.

Bits of pasta stick to Khal's face and upper chest and the look he gives me is absolutely murderous.

Yep.

I was going to die today.

Behind me, I here Nyam clear his throat.

"Why. . ." He seems at a loss for words, "Why did you do that?"

"The pasta had garlic in it." I say this with as much calm as I can muster.

I look to the still fuming Khal. Aside from being pissed, he seems perfectly fine. Maybe garlic doesn't work on vampires? Well. . . it had been roasted though, maybe it needed to be fresh?

"For the last damn time, I'm a god, not a vampire!" Khal explodes.

"Then prove it."

"*Prove it?*" He asks incredulously, while gesturing to his seven-foot, crimson frame.

He's back to looking at me like I'm too stupid to live. Clearly, he doesn't get it. I believed he wasn't human (he was a giant, red monster, for fuck's sake), I just didn't believe he was *a god*.

"Yes, prove it."

"How?" He's back to growling his words and a tick is working the left side of his face.

"Bring my parents back."

He doesn't immediately respond, like he's trying to mull out an appropriate answer. Finally, he just gives up and shouts:

"I can't do that! I'm not-"

"*God?*" I supply sardonically for him, cutting him off.

Khal snarls and starts walking towards me. Out of the corner of my eye, Nyam steps forward until he's in front of me. He reaches back to protectively tuck me aside before his body is engulfed in a blinding light. And then everything goes white. I hear voices shouting at each other in a strange tongue. I look wildly around, but everything remains blank.

CHAPTER 25

ZAHRA

I'm not going to panic.

I'm not going to panic.

I'm panicking!

I'm blind!

Ohmygod. . .

"Breathe, Zahra," I hear Kane croon, as I feel him scoop me up. "It will pass in a moment."

I struggle to control my breathing. The surrealism is finally wearing off and reality is crashing down on me. A million questions flit through my mind and I focus on them, instead of the mind-boggling paradigm shift that is now called 'my life'.

"What are they saying?" I croak to Kane.

"Can you not understand them?" He asks.

"No. They aren't speaking English."

I still cannot see anything, but turn my face towards Kane's voice. I feel like a china doll in his arms. . . I probably look like one, too. When Kane does not say anything, I fling my hands out sightlessly, until I'm touching his face, reading his expression like Braille. His brow is furrowed, as if in confusion.

"What?" I ask when he still does not answer me.

"You understood Khal in your dreams, but you cannot now?"

Oh- Khal and Nyam were speaking. . .*Godian? Godese?* Huh, that is weird. Why would I understand it then and not now? Come to think of it, this is what Illu and Uryn had been speaking to one another, other than Russian. I had instinctively recognized it, but couldn't recall where I had heard it at the time. Now I know: from my dreams. . . except, were they really even dreams? My brain hurts too much to even begin to ponder that bizarre twist.

"What are you guys going to do with me?" I whisper to Kane.

He gives me a reassuring squeeze.

"We are not going to hurt you, I promise."

Good answer- no, best answer.

"Ok, but *what do you want with me?*"

I'm perplexed. . . I cannot figure out my purpose in all of this. . . When dream Khal was with those women, he was

216

doing something to them, I could feel it. . . do they want to do that to me?

"What was Khal doing to those women in my dreams?"

"Feeding." Kane whispers back.

The fuck you say- *feeding*?! Kane must be able to sense my anxiety levels shooting up, because he rubs my back soothingly, while clarifying:

"We must feed off of human souls to fuel our immortality. It's the only thing that can replenish us in this realm."

"I'm sorry, my ears must be malfunctioning, too. . . did you say you *eat humans*?"

Kane chuckles, like I'm amusing.

"No, *lahela'iki*, not 'eat' as you humans consume food, but rather, garner sustenance from the person's soul. It does not *hurt* them."

He places a strange emphasis on the word 'hurt' and I sense the omission in his explanation.

"But does it harm them?"

I feel Kane shift underneath me and he does not answer me immediately. Almost reluctantly, he says:

217

"Anytime someone takes a piece of your soul, they are not doing you a favor."

Yeah, I can imagine having an intact soul would be a pretty big deal. So, they consume souls to survive, huh? They're demons. Figures. Well, I had Mio and Nyam pegged. I'm damn good at that.

"What are you thinking, *lahela'iki*?"

"Khal is right. You guys aren't vampires. You're demons."

Kane chuckles darkly and it does funny things to my insides.

"No, we are *gods*. We embody a lot of traits similar to your earthly, monstrous creations, but only because we *are* them. It's how humans compartmentalize our existence, by explaining us away as vampires, demons, fairies, and so forth."

His deep voice makes me squirm in his lap. He firmly quells my movements with strong hands.

"Sit still," he commands gruffly, his sternness taking me by surprise.

On the scale of 'how fucked up is it', what would you rate me sitting in Kane's lap wishing he would finger me in front of a room full of gods? Only like a two, right? Not that fucked up? Because I seriously want Kane to finger-bang me. Who knew he had an alpha side? But I dig it.

(Side note: I need help, don't I?)

Changing the topic so I do not mount the giant god, I ask:

"Why can't I see?"

"What do you think happens when you look at the sun?"

"What?"

"We are *planetary gods*. Nyam is the sun. His light has temporarily blinded you."

"The sun is a star. Not a planet." I state.

"Aren't you an *astrologist?*"

His voice echoes some of Khal's condescension from earlier. Great, even Kane thinks I'm lacking brain cells. Well, I might call the sun a planet when reading charts, but in the real world, it was still technically a star. I don't respond, because colorful spots are beginning to appear on the blank canvas of my vision. *As if I had been staring at the sun too long.* Slowly, my eyes begin to blink back into focus the world around me. Khal has shifted back to his. . . uh. . .

earthly form? And Nyam is not glowing. Phew. This situation is fucked up, I tell you.

I circle back to my original question, which I realize Kane never answered. I look to the others.

"What do you guys want from me?"

Arawn surprises me by answering:

"We want you to read our charts, compare them, and find our balance, as you said we had."

It's difficult to understand him around his Irish burr making me want to jump him. Ok, so they just want some chart interpretations? Seems easy enough. . .

"And you'ren't going to eat my soul. . . or me?"

"We won't touch your soul." Arawn states confidently.

"But we are definitely going to *eat you*," Mio adds wickedly.

Khal and I both groan, but the others grin at Mio's innuendo.

"Go now. Do your work. And don't tell anyone about us." Caed is still wearing a small smile, but his words are laced in steel. "We'll be watching."

I cringe as I quickly leave.

I needed to start a vice to help me cope with this shit.

222

CHAPTER 26

PLUTO

"You told her too much information, brother." I scold Jupiter.

While Saturn and Sun bickered back and forth, I tuned-in to the conversation between Zahra and the god of expansion. Jupiter casually shrugs, seemingly unaffected by my concern.

"She was curious. I had to give her some explanation. I know you think she's fatuous, but she isn't, really. If we don't want her figuring this out on her own, or worse, prying into our affairs, then I had to give her something. If only to pacify her for the time being."

I stand to pace. He's right, if course. Zahra is not stupid. We must never underestimate her. Because underneath this human shell lurks a very devious being. I look back to Jupiter.

"She couldn't understand Saturn and Sun just now?"

"No. . . I think it has to do with her repressed memories. When she was not consciously aware, I think her brain automatically switched into our language. This is why she understood Saturn when she was astrally projecting."

"This is not good," I muse. "This means either she does remember something or her memory is coming back."

"I suppressed her subconscious from being able to recall any further information," Neptune interjects.

"When?"

"Yesterday. . . when she was with Uranus."

I raise my brows, but Mercury and Sun are grinning like maniacs. I had forgotten how they were together. Being so far out of orbit from the others occasionally left me disconnected. My curse taking over does not help, but I must remain focused if I'm going to be any use to us.

"What did you two do?" I demand, looking at the inner planetary gods.

"We didn't do anything. Maybe you should be asking the Geminis what they did, instead." Sun taunts.

Neptune is not making eye-contact anymore and Uranus is glaring at Mercury and Sun, as if this is all their fault. I don't doubt that it's. Saturn huffs an irritated breath.

"Elucidate." He orders, looking at Uranus.

Bad idea. The god of autonomy does not like being told what to do. His twin steps in to intervene. Mars looks disappointed. Sick bastard is always looking for a fight.

224

"Uranus was. . . talking to Zahra yesterday, when he recommended that I suppress her memories from resurfacing while getting some information from her."

"What kind of information," I ask.

"Doesn't matter. We didn't learn anything, anyway," Neptune says.

"You two fucked her, didn't you?" Mars jeers.

"Not with our dicks," Uranus crudely rejoins.

"And she remembered, even though you blocked everything, and came here pissed and looking for answers," Saturn surmises.

Mars laughs out loud.

"No wonder she kept demanding we not touch her."

The twins look irritated.

"She shouldn't have remembered," Neptune grumbles.

"Exactly," I interpose. "Who has been able to override your 'suggestions' before? We must have a care. She's growing stronger. Her memory will return soon. We need her to do those charts and quickly."

Everyone nods in agreement. I move to leave, but Mercury pauses me by asking:

"Why were you so sure we wouldn't sample her soul when she asked?"

"Because Lina does not have one."

I leave without a backward glance to that assertion.

ZAHRA

I meet Mary outside the Presidential Office when I'm leaving and she cuts me a surprised look.

"I didn't know you were coming in today."

I shrug noncommittally, not bothering to comment.

"Well, I'm glad. The boys explained their plans for your interim here while you work on their project. I have almost everything ready for you. . . the house, the keys, and Khal has offered you a vehicle, too."

I blink.

What is she talking about?

Oh- I forgot. . . Khal has a place for me to stay for the next couple of months. . . that conversation seems like a lifetime ago. . . my time in Minnesota seems like twenty lives ago. Could it really only have been four days since I was last there? My world got turned upside down in the span of *three days*. Well friends, my advice: don't get too comfortable in life. It's just waiting to dump you on your ass.

"Dear?" Mary looks at me, waiting.

"Uh, sorry?"

"I asked when you wanted to fly back to Minnesota to get your things?"

"Um, can I get back to you on that?"

"Of course. In the meantime, here is the house information." She hands me a manila envelope. "Oh, and don't forget tonight's Luau! It's at the resort at 7:15."

Fuck, the Luau. . . where I can get lei'd. I kind of think I do need to get laid. Maybe that can be my vice-indiscriminate sexual activity. Could be worse. . . I could be hooked on blow.

Perspective.

I thank Mary and leave. Once outside, I remember I didn't take the town car and I need to get a taxi. I hail one and quickly slip in. After I tell the driver where to go, I sit back and just. . . absorb. Monster Man was real. Vampires were real. Demons were real. Because apparently they were all gods. *God was real.* And there was more than one. . .

And they were all dudes.

Called that.

Again. (*In case you forgot, go back and see my first sidebar tangent.*)

The people back in my town would lose their shit if they knew the truth. Is this who we had been petitioning and paying homage to all those years? No wonder my prayers never got answered. Those dickbags have yet to be actually helpful towards me, unless it benefits them in some way. I think about them being gods. . . what does that even *really* mean? Obviously, it's not a religious thing, but that's all I really have to base my understanding of a god on. . .

I think of Khal as a human and as a ~~monster~~ god. I try to mentally assess whether there are any similarities between his earthly form and his godly one. . . then I mentally switch between fantasizing about getting screwed by his human side

228

and his god side. Would that count as two men or just one? I would Google it, but I doubt the search engine would have any answers. (Actually, knowing society today, there might actually be a thread somewhere in the internetverse on this very topic. Ok, I'm Googling it now.)

When I arrive at the resort, I grab a quick lunch at the organic little deli bar and head upstairs to my room. I decided on the ride I need to work on their charts. Before, it was going to be a mild chore, but now I think it might give me some answers about the eight of them. They are too interested in these chart interpretations. And about the moon. But why me? The question has been nagging me. . . anyone could read their charts, but I got the feeling my interpretations were. . . *more*. Something is going on and I'm going to find out what.

I pull out all seven charts and start isolating their moons. In every single one, the celestial crescent is either squared or opposed. I compare the charts manually, but find no common denominator. The moon makes a hard aspect to different planets. Jupiter, Mars, Mercury, and the sun are squared in four of the charts and Pluto, Neptune, Uranus, and Saturn are opposed in the other three charts. The outer planets seem more adversely aspected than the inner ones. I keep thinking. . .

What did Kane say about Nyam?

That he was the sun?

Did he mean *The Sun*?

'*We are planetary gods,*' is what Kane had said. . .

I realize I did not really process that information properly, but reflecting upon Nyam suddenly glowing bright and then actually blinding me makes the light click on in my astrological brain.

They were the planetary gods of the zodiac.

That is why Kane questioned me when I insisted the sun was a star, not a planet. He expected me to view everything through an astrologist's lens. . . or needed me to, in this case. Using this newfound insight, I grab Nyam's chart and see it's his sun that squares the moon. I grab my phone and shoot a quick text to Khal:

ME: *Who are you?*

I probably should have explained myself better. He responds a second later.

KHAL: *I'm who am.*

What a fucking smartass.

ME: *I know you're 'god', which one, though?*

I almost tack on 'dick', but think better of it. They really haven't demonstrated the full extent of their capabilities, and I should probably tread lightly until I have a better understanding of them.

KHAL: *I'm the god of discipline.*

Wow, when you just read that abstractly. . . it kind of sets your mind up to picture some stuff, right? Naughty stuff. Like *I-have-been-a-bad-girl-and-need-disciplined-meow* kind of stuff. Let's just take a moment to enjoy that mental image before moving along. . .

Damn, I got sidetracked again. We need to stay on pace, this is some serious shit we are in. . . no need to point out there is no 'us' in this situation. . . it's all on me. That makes me a sad panda. I need a physical support team to help me through this troubling time. Ok, back on track. I text Khal a confirmation question.

ME: *So, you're Saturn?*

KHAL: *Obviously.*

I'm surprised his mother didn't strangle him as a child. (Did gods have mothers? I'm guessing no, since Khal is alive.)

ME: *And the others?*

KHAL: *Figure it out.*

AAAAAAAAAHHHHHHHHHHHHHHH! That man is the most frustrating non-human I have ever met. And that is saying something because the other seven are pretty damn vexing as well.

ME: *Must you be so hard?*

I could have kicked myself the minute I sent it. I meant *difficult.*

KHAL: *Apologies. I thought you liked it when I was hard.*

Jesus, even sexting, this man was uptight.

KHAL: *Or do you just like it hard?*

I almost choke on my sweet tea.

ME: *You really need a primer in digital conversations. Usually one adds an emoji or something to indicate they are joking.*

KHAL: *I wasn't joking.*

Was he *flirting* with me? I try to decipher his meaning and motives. . . Probably best not engage him further. . .

ME: *I like it when you're hard and when you give it to me harder.*

. . . I'm really bad at taking my own good advice.

KHAL: *I'll remind you of this when you're bent over my desk.*

. . . I think my brain succumbed to mental combustion. . . My vagina is now running this show. Before I can even formulate a response to send back to him, Khal sends me a new text.

KHAL: *See you tonight.*

I'm not going to survive the next two months, am I?

(That was a rhetorical question.)

Ok, so Nyam is the sun. I look at Nyam's chart as a whole, instead of just focusing on the moon and see that his sun is the strongest energy in the wheel. I think of when I first assessed the charts, trying to discern whose was whose. . . Each one had a ruling planet or sign whose energy reigned supreme. For Khal, it was definitely Saturn. I remember it being conjunct his MC and his rising sign was Capricorn. So much discipline. (His neurotic compulsions make sense. Good thing he doesn't have a strong Virgo, his OCD would be off the charts!)

233

Caed's chart was all fire, with a rising Aries and Mars in the exalted sign and house. . . I think of his turbulent disposition. . . Ok, so Caed is Mars. I look to the others and make similar connections. Mio is Mercury, Kane is Jupiter, Arawn is Pluto. . . but the twins are who? I think of them and their names. *Uryn and Illu.* Uryn sounds like Uranus. . . which means Illu is Neptune. I look at their charts with the moon. . . each planet representative of their godhood harshly aspects the earthly satellite.

That was the connection.

Unfortunately, it did nothing for helping me understand what those eight were up to. If anything, it made me even more confused and curious. I go round and round, looking at their charts with their planets in isolation and as a whole. Nothing resoundingly analogous stands out. . . the only consistent trait all eight men have is their Part of Fortune. They each have it in the sign of Virgo. But even their 'afflicted' moons do not have a lot in common. I don't know what I'm looking for and what they want me to find.

I pour over the charts for hours, until I realize it's almost 6:00 and I need to get ready. I change into a little, floral sundress that has an island flare. Perfect for a Luau. I wear my hair down and grab my sandals, without putting them on. I better go find the guys and tell them what I have

234

found. I think back to Khal's texts. Damn him for working me up. I definitely need to find a fuck buddy at this party. . . *a human one.*

CHAPTER 27

ZAHRA

The Luau looks to be in full swing when I arrive, although it's not even a quarter after seven. Located in a private pavilion at the back end of the resort, there are cheery strings of lights, women dressed in grass skirts handing out leis, and waiters milling around with drink trays. I decide to snag a glass of. . . champagne? White wine? Fuck if I know. It looks so pretty. . .

It tastes worse than my detox tea.

How can people stand this stuff?

I meander around, taking in the scene. Mary wasn't kidding about this being a traditional Luau; aside from the dancers and flower necklaces, there is a giant pig skewered over an open fire- roasting whole hog, and a long buffet table of traditional Hawaiian dishes. The booze I probably wouldn't do, but I could push past my comfort zone to try some new foods. I mean, I've had two three-ways in that past couple of days, I should be down for trying new things, right?

"Zahra, dear! You're here! What do you think?"

Behind me, Mary is smiling that thousand-watt grin. She's dressed in a wrap dress with printed shells and fish. I don't know how old she's exactly. . . but *she has it going on.* Note to self: look like Mary when I get older.

"It looks phenomenal. . . I feel like I'm actually in Hawaii."

Mary beams, like I just gave her the highest compliment. Seeing as she probably coordinated this whole thing, I probably did.

"Follow me. I'll introduce you to some of the other gals."

I walk behind Mary as we weave through the crowd, until we come to a group of girls who look to be around my age. They are sporting short, tight dresses and heavily made-up faces. A few teeter in their heels and I wonder if it's from the shoes or too much liquid courage.

"Zahra, this is Beth, Amanda, Trisha, Megan, and Jessica. They work in Human Relations and Marketing."

I give a little wave because the girls do not seem nearly as friendly as Mary, if their derisive looks are any hint.

"Oh, there's Roger from Accounting. I'll be right back."

Mary gives me a nudge towards the girls and then darts off to catch up with the man walking away. I look back at the set of women and notice they are not even trying to hide the sneers from their faces now. One girl (Megan, maybe?) looks mildly nicer (which is not saying much) and asks with curiosity:

"So you're the new one?"

"Ummmmmm. . . what?"

"The new 'flavor' of the week, she means," Beth interjects cuttingly.

"Uhhhhhh. . ."

I'm not getting any articulation points in this conversation, but what the hell are they talking about?

"*She came with Mary,*" Jessica whispers, like I can't hear her.

"Is there a problem with that?" I demand.

I'm all for turning my back on the patriarchy and reforming the bonds of womanhood again, but I'm not letting these little bitches throw Mary under the bus. That woman has done nothing but help me. She's the only true point of pleasantness in this *fiasco.* The girls seem to step down at my display of bark.

239

"No- no, there is nothing wrong with that. It's just. . . the, ah, guys do not generally let anyone work with them unless they are *family*." Jessica says this like she swallowed something sour.

Clearly someone is pissed about not being upper-level management.

Did that mean one of the boys was related to Mary, then?

I notice the girls are still waiting for some sort of explanation for my presence at the office.

"Yeah, I'm, um. . . a sister."

They all give me varying looks of 'no fucking way'.

"You're actually siblings with one of them?" Trisha asks this like I'm nuts.

Maybe I should have said distant cousin?

"Well, the brother got all the good looks," Jessica chimes in again with her faux whisper.

That's it. I'm going to purposely stab these whores. No accident about it this time. I'm looking around for a suitable shank (the little cocktail umbrellas in their drinks might work), when someone slings an arm around my shoulders.

"Our parents used to say the same thing,"

It's Caed.

He's the epitome of the leisurely gentlemen dressed in board shorts and a casual button down. He has a drink in his right hand and looks like he spent the entire day on the beach. (He didn't. Part of it was spent mouth fucking some girl on Khal's desk in the Presidential Office. I remember. I walked in on it. . . you know, right before I learned they were all monsters, I mean gods.)

The girls titter behind their glasses, laughing at my expense.

"Isn't that so, *little* sister?" Caed goads, picking up his antagonism from earlier.

"Yep, you got all the looks, *dick* brother, but I got all the brains."

The girls gasp at my irreverence.

"Oh, did I say 'dick brother', I meant 'dear brother'. Freudian slip."

Caed looks torn between laughter and vexation. From the bulging outline in the front of his shorts, he also seems to be getting some sick pleasure from this whole thing. My mind recalls a hazy dream of being in the office

241

with the eight, but not really there. . . A thought of Caed being a sexual deviant flits across my memories. . . What were they talking about in that dream? Because now I'm not so sure it was one.

Caed distracts me by dragging me away from the girls. I don't bother saying good-bye.

"Making friends?" He asks me.

"Yep, I'm reclaiming the bonds of womanhood and then we are going to overthrow all the dicks at corporate."

He looks at me askance, trying to gauge whether I was being truthful or not. I just smile amiably at him.

"Would you like a drink," he offers politely.

"No, thanks- I don't drink."

"Yes, you do."

I grind to halt and yank my arm out of his hand.

"No. I. Don't." I state through gritted teeth.

He seems confused.

"Are you abstaining or. . . I don't know. . . a recovering addict?"

His high opinion of me really is doing fuzzy things inside my head. Oh wait- that's just the anger sharks swimming to get out.

"No, I'm not a recovering addict, you dickhead! And I'm not 'abstaining'," I take a page from Khal's book and add some finger quotes. "I just don't like alcohol. *Is that a problem?!*"

Caed looks at me like I'm a loose cannon. Which is rich, considering he's the god of violent pastimes.

"No." He mutters something under his breath. . . it sounds like 'you used to drink'. What the fuck does *that* mean? We walk a little further until we come to a section roped off from the rest of the pavilion. Of course these eight would have a 'VIP section' at a company party.

"Too good to hang with your employees?" I snipe.

"Play nicely," Caed warns, before escorting me over to the other seven and a few other men I have not met.

CHAPTER 28

ZAHRA

Khal flashes me a charming smile when I get closer. It's very *un-reassuring.*

"Ah, Zahra, you look lovely this evening," Khal compliments. "Allow me to introduce you to some potential investors- we are looking into expanding our properties. This is Mr. Julio Alvaro, Mr. Brett Michaels, and Mr. Ian Figgenbaum."

He points to the men from left to right, who all nod their heads accordingly to me.

"And this is Zahra Delsol, our resident metaphysical specialist."

I arch a brow. He makes it seem like I'm an old member of the team. Whatever. I politely shake hands with the three men, watching warily as they openly assess me.

"You're Latina, then, *señorita?*" Julio asks with a husky inflection to his words. A fellow Spanish speaker.

"Mis abuelos paternales nacieron en España, pero la familia de mi mama fue de Escocia"

"¿Fue?"

"Yes, I don't have any living relatives that I know of actually." I answer to his question about what happened to my mother's side of the family.

Beside me, Arawn's and Khal's eyebrows are doing Stephen Colbert impressions. Ha! I'm a lot more awesome than they thought. (Not that awesome though- I took Spanish in college as my 'ancestral language'. I got pretty good at it, enough for basic conversations, but that is all.)

"My apologies for bringing up such a delicate matter, señorita." Julio bows his head in contrition.

He appears to be in his late thirties, like Brett and Ian, and would be extremely good-looking if my eight bosses were not loitering around, ruining the view. I attempt to block the others out and focus on Julio's dark eyes. I could do worse for my vice. . .

"No apologies necessary, Mr. Alvaro," I lean in a bit as I say this and seductively nip my bottom lip.

A stern clearing of the throat behind me has Julio snapping to attention and me reluctantly pulling back. I try to not turn around and glare at the jerk behind me. This is payback for me being their cock block, isn't it? Ian tries to smooth things over by asking:

"Metaphysical specialist, eh? What does that entail?"

246

"Oh, all kinds of new-agey stuff," I respond before Khal can say anything better. "I do energy healing and intuitive readings using astrology, numerology, or tarot."

"Astrology?"

"Yep, like natal chart interpretations and more advanced chart readings, if the client is interested. It's a tool to help people understand the deeper levels of their psyche."

The three don't look impressed, per se, but intrigued. I get that a lot. Even if someone thinks it's a load of crock, they still want to know about it (*so they can later put you in your place of how that cannot be it*).

"A tool, how?" Brett asks.

"Well, for example, I'm a Virgo Rising and have a Capricorn Sun, so I'm very detail-oriented and work driven. . . but my sun is in my 5th house, the house of creative expression and fun, so my work needs to be something authentic to my nature and something I enjoy."

The men seem a little more enthralled than before and I decide to restart flirting with Julio. I bat my lashes at him, as I ask:

"When's your birthday?"

"El siete de agosto," he answers.

"The 7th of August? That makes you a Leo. I can't really say much more without seeing the rest of your chart, but you're confident, creative, and *passionate*. Leo rules the 5th house, where my sun is. . . it's also the house of love and sexual attractions."

I think I once upon a time said that *subtlety was the lost art*. . . clearly it was lost on me, too, because I'm not even trying to hide my attempts at seduction anymore. And by looking at his grin, Julio is game.

"The house of love and sexual attraction, you say?" Nyam comments, joining the conversation. Fuck me, what is he up to? Of course he knows what the 5th house entails. . . he's the exalted ruler of it!

"You know, I would love to tell you more. Want to go sit down with me?" I send Julio a sultry grin to accompany my invitation.

I need to leave before Nyam says something to fuck up my chances.

"Are you taking Brett and Ian with you?" Nyam asks innocently enough.

"Ah. . . if they would like to join us. . . they can. . ."

"Well, I know how you like being with more than one man at a time."

248

Brett spits his colorful drink down the side of Ian's face and bends over, choking, as Julio whacks his back. I glare at Nyam. Did I say I needed to leave before he said something?

Too late. Too fucking late.

"Screw you, Nyam. I have never been with multiple men at one time *before* this week. You, Mio, and the twins are the ones who fucked me by initiating me!"

Brett chokes some more. I should probably clarify.

"I didn't actually have sex with any of them. . . I mean, I tried to blow Mio-"

I'm not helping myself, am I?

"Shut the front fucking door," Caed says (I don't think he got the point of that phrase). "You *blew* Mio? I don't recall you ever offering to suck my dick."

"I can't suck your dick- I'm your sister, apparently!"

Brett might now be dying. Ian and Julio quickly yank him out of the secured area and back into the crowd of mingling Miraval employees. I don't think Khal is going to get to expand his properties with them. . . whoops. But when I look back at the severe god of control, he's grinning at me. Glad I could be their entertainment.

"Are you twits done tormenting me? I actually have something useful to tell you."

This gets their attention. Khal motions for us to follow him and we walk away from the party, deeper into the darkness of the night.

"What have you learned, *lahela'iki*?" Kane asks.

I explain to them about how their individual godhoods are directly linked to their afflicted moons and how their representative namesake rules their charts. None of them seem overly surprised at this, so I continue. I have not started in finding the overall balance in their charts, but I did cross-reference them to find similarities. Since I don't know what I'm looking for in particular (hint, hint, guys), I did a general assessment. The only parallel between the seven charts is their Part of Fortune, all in Virgo.

"What is this Part of Fortune," asks Illu.

"Well, let me first explain that the Part of Fortune comes from the Arabic parts, also called lots. These were first introduced into astrology in Arabia in the late Middle Ages. They do not represent physical points in the sky, but rather are mathematically derived from three points in the chart, such as planets or angles. The distance between two points is added or subtracted to the position of the third to

250

come up with the degree and sign of the part. For the Part of Fortune, depending upon whether you were born in the day, with your sun above the horizon line, or at night, with your sun below the horizon line, you calculate an equation using your ascendant, or rising sign, along with your sun and moon." I stop to see whether they are still following me.

No one looks lost and Uryn nods to encourage me to keep talking.

"Ok, so because the Part of Fortune is derived from the placements of the Sun, Moon, and Ascendant, it represents a macrocosm of your ego, unconscious, and personality and is translated into the overall health and fortune of a person. Basically, it's like your 'good luck' sign in your chart- even more so than Jupiter, where a person experiences abundance or blessings."

"Blessings. . ." Kane contemplates.

"As in the opposite of a curse?" theorizes Arawn.

"Ah, I suppose the antonym to a blessing would be a curse and vice versa." I offer.

"That is excellent. Thank you, Zahra." Khal commends.

I preen a little under his praise.

"If we were at the office, I would bend you over my desk like you want."

I'm back to glaring at him.

"Are you fucking kidding me? First she's blowing Mio and now you get to bend her over your desk. I guess it's my turn to hold down the girl." Caed says this all too conversationally.

I look over at the twins and silently beg them to keep their mouths shut. Luckily, they seem willing not to kiss and tell. . . for now. I need to get out of here. I look back to the Luau, now in full swing, with male dancers performing on a stage, juggling sticks of fire.

"Alright, well, I'm going to go. I'll work some more on your charts later. Do you want me at the office tomo- *shit!*"

The guys look at me, wondering what I'm swearing about now. I'm such a professional.

"I forgot I had my flight home tomorrow. I was supposed to get back to Mary about going home to sort things. . . you know, for the next couple of months. What should I do?"

"It's already taken care of, *mon coeur*."

"What?" I ask Nyam, bewildered.

"Stay through the weekend. We will switch out your flights and you can go home for a day or two next week. That way, you can keep working on the charts and apprise us in person about the progress."

"Ok, how are going to change my flight so late?"

"We're *gods*, remember?" He winks at me.

I roll my eyes.

He's definitely the sun: *all ego.*

CHAPTER 29

JUPITER

"May I come with you?" I ask Zahra, before she can go.

"Sure," she answers easily.

Of all of us, she seems most at ease with me. . . given her past interactions with the others, I can understand why.

"I actually was going to take a small stroll. . ."

"A walk around the resort would be nice; it has been too long since I last explored it."

She gives a nod and we skirt around the Luau pavilion to the secluded path that winds around the resort. Even though there are lamp posts dotting the area, everything is shrouded in shadows, due to the new moon not casting any natural light. We walk in amicable silence, until Zahra whispers:

"Can I ask you something?"

I hear the heaviness in her question and know it goes beyond something trivial, possibly beyond personal.

"My mother always said you could ask, but it did not guarantee an answer. I cannot stop your questions, *lahela'iki.* . ."

"But you cannot say whether you can answer them or not. That is what I should have asked. If you can answer something. . . actually *somethings* for me. . ."

It figures she's riddled with questions. I do not underestimate Zahra's astuteness, though, as knowledge in her hands could prove dangerous.

"What do you wish to know?"

"What can you tell me?"

I let out a laugh. Clever girl.

"How about an exchange?" I propose.

The others have used their wiles to acquire information from her, perhaps I could use her curiosity to gather some as well.

"An exchange. . . meaning?"

"I'll tell you something if you tell me something."

"Uh. . . what do you want to know?"

"Tell me something. . . private. . . something personal."

I figure if there is any clue that she's unaware of from her previous life, it would be through something of this nature.

"Huh. . . well, you already know I donated my vibrator to Goodwill- *by accident.* Personal like that?"

I tuck my head to my chest and just laugh. This girl is something else.

"I was thinking more along the lines of private or personal thoughts."

"Oh," she says quietly. I hear the trepidation in her voice. . . I might be on to something.

"You can tell me. I would never judge you. And in return, I'll tell you something about us." I'm taking a gamble, as the guys all agreed that no more information regarding us or our past lives should be divulged to Zahra. But if she told me something useful. . .

"Earlier today, when I was in your lap- ah, blinded, you got stern with me, and with your deep voice, it made- I mean I wanted- no, I thought about you fingering me in front of all the other guys." She blurts out.

Horror washes over her face and she clamps both hands over her mouth. I'm rooted to my spot, having stopped walking during her confession, and work to control my body. As gods, we have infinite memories, and I can recall exactly the moment she's referring to from earlier today. She had been squirming in my lap, sending a fissure of pleasure to my groin. I had halted her movements, almost becoming rough in my effort to stop her before I embarrassed myself. At the time, I was worried I had been too gruff with her. . . apparently not. I express this previous concern.

"Oh- no." She blushes. "I kind of liked it when you got all firm with me. . ."

No wonder we are all drawn to her. She appeals to our domineering tendencies, bred into us since the dawn of time.

Zahra continues, "I guess it just floored me, is all. . . the others act all alpha, ya know, but you seem so gentle and serene, I guess it just took me by surp-"

Her voice cuts off when I push her body roughly into the darkened alcove, across from where we had been standing. Not giving either one of us a chance to think, I crush my mouth to hers and let go of the reigns holding me back. Like Saturn, I have always kept a tight leash on my inner emotions and desires. Not necessarily because of the same consequences Saturn experiences, but because of my never-ending role as peacekeeper and the stigma that has come with it. I'm the perpetual 'good guy'. I'm expected to hold back, to sacrifice.

No longer.

CHAPTER 30

JUPITER

In all my eons of existence, there has only been one woman: Lina. After her curse and ultimatum, I made my peace with the situation. For this reason, I do not think the curse has affected me as strongly, as I have not fought against it, like the others. Instead, I embraced it as my reality and accepted its presence in my life. Being the largest and most benign planet has allowed me all this time to not feed from another and so I have not let that part of the curse imprecate me. And while I have my urges and desires, they were easy to repress in light of the situation.

But that was before Zahra.

Her admission broke my control and I burn to have her. I'm like the raging storm of my namesake, consuming everything she offers. She's so small against me, barely coming up to the middle of my chest, for I'm indeed a giant, even in human form. Both my hands span the entirety of her waist and hoist her forcibly against me, drinking in her whimpers when my tongue thrusts against hers savagely.

"Lift your dress up," I command brusquely.

I have her seated on the little ledge of the recessed wall, a precarious balance made only possible by my strong body stabilizing hers upward. She hesitates to comply and I pinch her chin to get her attention.

"I said lift your dress up. I'll not be asking again, *lahela'iki.*"

"O-o-o-o-kay," her voice wobbles out uncertainly.

"Answer only with 'yes sir' or 'no sir', understood?"

Her eyes widen, but she obeys.

"Yes, sir."

I'm so hard, I'm about to burst out of my patterned surf trunks I wore for the party. I watch as she slowly pulls the dress up until I can see the scrap of lace covering her core. Even in the dim light, I can see it's soaked through.

"Now, spread your legs."

When she doesn't say anything, I reach out and ruthlessly twist my thumb over her clit. She lets out a surprised yelp.

"Answer me!" I thunder.

"Yes, sir!" She all but sobs.

"Good girl."

I run my finger up and down the seam of her sex, making her moan and push against me harder. When she begins to pant erratically, I hook her panties with my finger and tug, until the pathetic excuse for underwear is in tatters around us.

"Touch yourself for me."

I catch her eye while she debates whether to follow my order or not. I lift a brow in challenge. One thing I have learned about Zahra- she does not step down from a dare. I'm using that to my advantage. As expected, her fingers go to her dripping pussy. . . what I did not expect is her maintaining eye contact as she slowly begins to fuck herself. In my peripheral, I can see her slender, white fingers slip inside the delicate pink flesh of her sex. Unable to hold back, I slide one of my own digits next to hers, until we are moving in tandem. One of my fingers is two of hers in size and is a tanned and callused contrast against the soft perfection of her digits.

The only sound now is the harsh breathing escaping us both as we work towards her release. I clamp back down on her clit, working it with my thumb and fore finger, while still keeping pace with my index finger inside of her. I hear her breath hitch as she climbs closer to her peak. I crook the digit deep inside her pussy while pressing hard against her sensitive nub and feel her beginning to unravel.

"*Not yet, Zahra.*"

I bring her to the top, before pulling back and repeating the process. Her legs are shaking and she's barely touching herself anymore. I take pity on her.

"Come for me, Zahra."

And she does. With a magnificent cry, she tilts her head back against the wall and gives a final, brutal thrust into my hand. Her body is bowed towards me, contorted in pleasure. Slowly, she comes down from her high, although her breathing is still coming in fitful gasps. Without warning, she pushes me away from her to slip to the ground. Once she's kneeling before me, she arches her head back to look at me while slowly stroking my erection.

"Fuck me. Make me come again." She says this on a breathless command.

I lift a brow. Her orgasm has made her brazen.

"Are you topping from bottom?" I ask smoothly.

Her forehead puckers in confusion. While naturally submissive, she has obviously never been in a dominant relationship.

"What?"

I grasp her long hair in my fist and tug until her back bends.

"Who is in charge here?"

"Yo-you-you're, sir." Comes her quavering answer.

She's learning.

"Exactly. So do you get to make demands?"

"No, sir. I just tho-"

"Undo my pants."

I release her hair so she can lean forward and do as I have requested. She doesn't stop until the full length of my cock is exposed to the night air. I can feel her breath against me, her lips a whispers-length away.

"Now, *fuck me* until *I* come."

I take hold of her long locks once more, so I can control her motions. Fisting her tresses, I angle her mouth over the crown of my cock. Poised over the tip, she snakes out a tongue to lick the pre-cum leaking from me, her eyes watching me as she attempts to take some control. Definitely topping from bottom, but she would understand soon enough. Narrowing my eyes, I unexpectedly push myself into her mouth, slamming my length and girth to the back of her throat. She gags at the invasion. Her eyes are now watering and overflowing down her face, but they convey that she gets the message.

I relent marginally, and start thrusting slowly, simply enjoying the feeling of her tongue washing over my dick. She makes a humming noise and I growl, feeling the vibrations pulse down through my balls. Her tiny hands come up to wrap around me and I know I should not let her or she'll never learn her lessons, but I realize she's acting on instinct, not a need to control the situation. So I allow her hands to work me up and down, synchronously following the movements of her mouth.

I try to keep control, but I can feel my orgasm barreling down my spine. It has been too long. Zahra's hands are moving at a frantic pace and I feel my balls tighten. Around a mouthful of cock, I hear her say:

"Come for me, Kane."

I roar in pleasure and irritation as I do just that. Zahra swallows down every last drop as I come in jets over her lapping tongue. She purrs happily, drinking me in, relishing in her little victory. She waited until the last possible moment to give me that command, knowing I was already going to come. I would let her think she had won, but in the end, I would be the one savoring her punishment.

266

I yank her delicate wrists until she's standing before me. She keeps her eyes downcast and attempts to look demure. Vixen. The question is should I punish her now or later? Of course, she's expecting my retaliation now. . . possibly even hoping for it. Zahra Delsol is quite the little deviant masochist. Wait until Caed finds out. I silently chuckle; perhaps I should let *him* dole out her punishment. I can see the triumph in Zahra's eyes when I do nothing to reprimand her. I smirk, later could not come soon enough.

CHAPTER 31

ZAHRA

I can't help the look of smug satisfaction from crossing my face when Kane does nothing. I needed to Google 'topping from bottom', but I figure it means something along the lines of trying to take control. . . well, from where I stand, it looks like I just topped the shit out of my place from bottom. But Kane does not look ruffled at my gloating. In fact, he looks entertained, like he knows something I do not. . . maybe I'm celebrating prematurely? I'm afraid to ask now. He grins, like he knows my quandary, tugging my wrists higher. Something catches his eye and I realize it's my tattoo.

"When did you get this?"

"My first year of college, when I started reading charts for money."

He seems confused by my response.

"It's not a Z?"

"No, it's the glyph for Virgo. But I stylized it so it would look like a cursive Z- you know, a 'two birds and one stone' kind of tattoo."

"I see, but Virgo is not your sun. . . you mentioned it was Capricorn?"

"Yes, I'm a New Year's baby, actually. See, the traditional name Sarah means *princess*, but mom named me after the Basque New Year. It's similar to ours, but celebrates the return of Venus in the heavens and is called 'Altizarra'. Anyway, I got the Virgo symbol because I'm Virgo Rising. Your ascendant is equally as important as your sun sign and is totally overlooked by everyone who doesn't practice astrology."

"Interesting- I mean about your name," He pauses, seeming hesitant before continuing, "Names are important to us as well and symbolize our status as gods on earth."

"What do you mean?"

"Well, remember when I told you my name was pronounced KAH-NAY?"

"Yes- and for the record, I offered to pronounce it that way, too!"

"I know, thank you, but as I said, no one has called me that for a long time. My people did, formerly, when I was still worshipped by them."

"Your people?"

"Yes, Kane is an island deity. While we are not originally from earth, humans turned us into terrestrial idols. And when the monotheistic religions took over, we became earth's monsters. So, once upon a time, I was Kane, the great father. . . I think you would know me better as Zeus."

"Zeus? The Greek *man-whore* Zeus?"

He tosses his head back to laugh out loud.

"Not everything is as it has been recorded. Remember, humans are only postulating about our existence and what we do, they do not know for certain, though."

I think this over. In Roman mythology, all the Greek gods were converted to become planetary deities. . . as is reflected in their names now. So Kane is Zeus, who is also Jupiter.

"Does that make Khal. . .ah-" My mythology facts are not up-to-date. I have always loved the stories, but it has been awhile. "Kronos!" I suddenly remember.

Kane nods his head in affirmation. The sickle tattoo suddenly comes to me and I recall Kronos' symbol being a sickle. I'm starting to piece together some of this confusing puzzle.

"And Khal's name also reflects this. . . actually all our names do. But Khal's last name, Al-Zahil, is derived from

271

his divinity. Zahil literally means *Saturn* in Arabic and Al comes from the Arabic name meaning *one God*, as in Allah. It also spills into other religious factions, such as Hebrew, where Al is El, as in Elohim. Khal is the first father."

"Khal's your *dad*?!"

Again, he laughs at me. Glad I'm so damn amusing.

"No, we are more like brothers, I guess you could say. Remember, this is just how humans have rationalized us."

I'm so eager to hear more, I'm practically bouncing up and down. I do not like mysteries. . . just tell me the ending, thank you.

"And the others?"

"What do you think?"

What is with these guys and making me work for shit? Just tell me. I'm lazy, dammit. Okay, let me think. . . astrology actually helps me understand language better and is directly linked to our everyday speech. In fact, you use these little paganisms every day. For example: Monday equals *moon* day, Sunday equals *sun* day (obviously, right), and Saturday equals *Saturn* day. Tuesday, Wednesday, Thursday, and Friday are based on Norse mythology, but correlate perfectly to their Greek/Roman counterparts, which can be seen in the French, Spanish, Italian, and Portuguese days of the week.

So, Tuesday is martes in Spanish and is linked to Mars, Wednesday is miércoles and is linked to Mercury, Thursday is jueves and is linked to Jupiter and Friday is viernes and is linked to Venus. Bet you didn't realize what an impious little heretic you really were, did you?

Sinner.

Not to mention how many times you have fantasized with me about Khal discipling us. . . you should probably go to confession soon. I won't waste my time. I think I'll bypass the confessor and go straight to the gods. *Exaggerated wink* This is where you remind me to focus.

Again.

Thank god (or do I thank them by name?) Kane cannot read minds. . . or can he? Yikes. I should ask him that later.

So, Mio's real name is Ermio Mercoledi. Mercoledi is Wednesday in Italian and is associated with Mercury. I think of Mercury cross-culturally. In Greek mythology, he's the messenger or Hermes. Pretty for sure *Ermio* is how you would say *Hermes* in Italian. I think of Nyam next. *Soley* means sun, but I'm unsure about his first name. I do not know enough Russian to riddle out the twins' names meaning, and Caed and Arawn are lost on me. I tell Kane my thoughts.

"Good, *lahela'iki*. Nyam's first name, Nyambe, comes from Western Africa, where he's known as the sun god by that appellation. As for the twins, their last name is Blitznetsy, meaning *Gemini* in Russian. Their first name correlates to their planet. Uryn comes from the Russian *uran*, meaning Uranus. And Illu means *illusion* in Russian, denoting one of Neptune's main characteristics. Arawn is the Welsh god of the underworld. Or Hades, as he's commonly known."

"Which translates to Pluto."

"Exactly. And Caed's name means *warrior*. And his planet is stated in his last name Marx. All pointing to Mars, or Aries, god of war."

This is some fascinating stuff. I should have brought a notebook. . . although, I don't know what I would have done with it when Kane made me fuck myself, so maybe it's good I did not have one.

"Are there no women gods. . . ah, I guess, goddesses?"

And just like that, Kane shuts down. Everything becomes shuttered and his eyes blank.

"We should get back to the party."

"Ok," I say meekly, unsure of what to do with his rapid change in disposition. "Actually, I'm kind of tired, I think I'll just go back to my room for the night."

Kane nods and abruptly walks away in the opposite direction.

What the fuck just happened?

URANUS

Jupiter finally joins us again, reeking of sex, but not saying a word. Sullen is not his normal look. . . but he definitely looks ill-humored. How he can smell like that and be in such a pissy mood, I cannot understand.

"We've been waiting for you," drawls Merc. "Have a good time with Zahra?"

"Fuck you. What are you waiting on me for?"

All of us wear varying looks of surprise. Jupiter is not the confrontational type. . . which means Zahra must have got to him. Saturn worried about this, but Jupiter is a big boy and can take care of himself.

"We have things to discuss. Important things, bigger than you getting off," Mars gibes.

In an instant, Jupiter morphs into his true form- an eight-foot titan with pale green skin, swirling red, brown, and white eyes, and otherworldly strength. He cocks back his fist and levels Mars with a single blow. The god of war is now sprawled in the grass, unconscious. Luckily, we are a distance from the party for anyone to notice the hulking leviathan possessing our normally placid friend. Sunny leans down to check Mars' pulse.

"Still alive!" He says in mock relief.

His comment seems to snap Jupiter back to reality and he changes back into his laid-back Hawaiian appearance. He looks troubled.

"What is wrong, *bratik*?" I ask.

We may not be blood brothers, like Neptune and I, but our physiology was derived from the same elemental energy of the universe. The blood of the cosmos runs through our veins and I love these men like family- we have been a unit since the beginning of time. They are my best friends and one's pain is all our pain.

Jupiter lets out a heavy sigh, "I'm sorry. . . I'm angry at myself. It's no excuse, though."

276

"Damn right it's no excuse, you oversized fucker," Mars grates from the ground, awake again.

Jupiter leans over to help him up.

"Well, what the fuck happened?" he demands, once standing again.

"Later. I'll tell you later. Again, I apologize."

Mars slaps a hand on his back, "No worries, bro. Good to see you again. . . when was the last time you changed? Not since Lina, no?"

I'm unsure if this is a jab at Jupiter, but he flinches anyway. I'm surprised Mars is not settling this with his fists. He has seemed a lot calmer recently. . . odd. Saturn, of course, steps up to take control and get us back on track.

"We were waiting for you to discuss what Zahra had said about our Part of Fortune. I think she may have inadvertently given us the key to understanding how to undo our curse."

"We agree it's the key. . . but how it unlocks anything for us, we have no clue," I add.

Jupiter is quiet while he mulls Zahra's words in his head. I hope he can shed some light onto the topic, because all we have been able to do is hit dead ends.

277

"I do not know. . . modern day astrology is so different from when we first came to earth and the humans began worshipping us. As Zahra said, they began adding things, like the lots, with no actual astronomical reference point. So, unlike us or the Minor Gods, there is no Part of Fortune for us to physically locate and question. Let's give Zahra a couple of days to see if she can give us any new insight."

"A sound plan. I'll update Zahra tomorrow and reschedule her flight." Saturn says.

"Just make sure she thinks we used our powers to do it," Sunny reminds.

"Who needs power when you have money?" Saturn rejoins.

"I know, but girls are turned on by power."

"I think they like money more," inserts Pluto.

"Sheilas love both. Throw a little money their way. . . display some power- not you, though, Jupiter. You keep your shit under wraps."

"I said I was sorry. I meant it, too."

"Yeah, well, you owe me one, man."

A strange smile grows takes over Jupiter's face.

278

"Actually, I have the perfect thing for you."

Mars perks up, intrigued by the look on Jupiter's face.

"What's that? It better be good. . ."

"I need you to discipline Zahra for me."

Merc lets out a whistle, while Mars shifts into Dom mode.

"What kind of punishment are we talkin'?"

I look to my twin. Neptune just rolls his eyes.

It always has been a competition to see who was more fucked up.

CHAPTER 32

ZAHRA

I wake Thursday morning to my phone dinging. I have a text from Khal. It says I have a return flight home scheduled for Saturday morning and to plan to be back here Monday night. In the meantime, I should spend my time analyzing the charts for balance and see if there is more similarity to everyone's Part of Fortune. Well, at least this would keep me busy. . . and hopefully keep my mind off Kane. . . what went wrong last night? Everything seemed to be going well- until I asked about girl gods.

Goddesses. . . I kind of preferred girl gods.

(You know how I like alliterations.)

Was this some unspoken bone of contention for the lot of them and I had inadvertently offended Kane by bringing it up?

Maybe there were no girl gods. . . maybe they had to slum it with us human gals and wished for more divine consorts.

Or maybe the girl gods got sick of their shit and left.

If I were a betting person, I would say it was the latter. Those eight were enough to drive any sensible vagina insane, even a deific vagina.

(Sidebar tangent: What does a heavenly vagina look like? Like perfectly pink, shrouded in celestial clouds and plated in gold? The infamous Fountain of Youth, forever gushing?)

(Sidebar tangent to a sidebar tangent: It's starting to feel really judgey on your end. Reign that shit in- we are restoring the ties of sisterhood and your censure has no place in this new system. Respect the sisterhood and the Trust Tree. And stop eyeballing my words like I'm batshit crazy- we both know you have wondered about girl god vaginas before this, thanks to Wonder Woman.)

Well, if I did learn a lesson last night, it was:

1. Use 'yes, sir' and 'no, sir' with Kane and
2. Do not ask about girl gods.

Whatever. They might call themselves gods, but having a penis made them no different from any other man. They blew hot, the blew cold, and right now, they could go blow each other because I'm over trying to figure them out. I have work to do. I pull back out their charts and double down. I cross-reference everything like a pro (because I totally am one), and let me tell you, doing a synastry reading for seven people is no easy feat. A lot of details, folks.

And that is what sets good astrologists from the great: the ability to read the details, but still see the big picture. It's easy to get caught up in the minutiae of a chart, until you're so mired in one piece of the wheel that you forget it takes three hundred and sixty degrees to make a full circle. Not this all-star astrologist. I totally can see the forest for the trees. (Did I finally use an everyday colloquialism correctly? If not, fuck it. . . That's the advice from my book *Fuck It: This Is My Life*- to just say 'fuck it' to what is not going your way. I love it and encourage you to use it, too.)

What I notice when I look at their afflicted moons is that the other planets seem to create a sort of 'safety net' around the planet being aspected. The other planets support the one being squared or opposed to the moon, but the moon is not offered similar backing in the charts. Interesting. If I were to take this literally, then I would read it as the guys help one another, but do not offer the moon the same defense. Who was the moon? Was it a real person, like the other eight. . . another planetary god?

Or was it a girl god?

The moon is always a feminine energy.

283

This is why Kane got so upset. A girl god fucked them. Obviously, if their afflicted moon is any indication.

Shit, I'm like Sherlock Holmes, Super Sleuth.

Actually, I'm probably more like Inspector Gadget, but let's not quibble over semantics.

Okay- so how do I bring this up to the guys? I'm pondering this new development when I get an incoming call from Khal.

"Ms. Delsol, how are things coming?" I'm *Ms. Delsol* again.

"Swimmingly."

"And have you found anything new?"

"Ah, yes, some minor things. . ."

"Such as?" But it comes across as 'stop wasting my time and tell me'.

I tell him what I have found- minus the part about asking if the moon is a girl god. Khal wonders if I can email over their charts, highlighting this new information.

"Sure, give me until tomorrow morning though, please."

"That's fine."

284

"Was there anything else, *Mr. Al-Zahir?*"

"Actually, yes. Firstly, don't call me that unless you want to get fucked from behind. Secondly, how do you calculate balance in a chart, overall?"

I know he asked me something. . . but I'm still hung up on the first part of his sentence. . . I get a mental image of him bending me over his desk, while Caed holds me down, and Khal slams into me brutally from behind while the other six watch. . . I must really have a thing for voyeurism I never knew about.

"*Zahra?*" Khal purrs from the other end of the line.

Dick. He knows exactly where my mind went and what his words did to me.

"What was the question again?"

I hear him give a low snigger at my lack of attention.

Do I still want to fuck these guys or just kill them?

Tough decision.

"I asked, *how do you calculate balance in a chart as a whole?*"

"Oh, well, I look at the elements and the modalities: the twelve signs of the zodiac are either fire, earth, air, or water and either cardinal, fixed, or mutable. If there is one weaker or less present than the others, I see how the stronger ones bring a semblance of balance to the chart. Of course, I assess opposite houses and opposites in general, as opposites balance- not attract. Like attracts like. And lastly, I look to the individual degrees of the planets and houses to find correspondence and equilibrium."

I hear him writing down what I have said.

"Thank you. I'll be waiting for those charts. Good day."

How can someone threaten to fuck me doggy style and say 'good day' in the same conversation?

Ridiculous man. . . god.

Man god. I like it. I'm coining it- that and *girl god.*

CHAPTER 33

ZAHRA

I'm debating about whether I want to send a new submission to Webster (for *man god* and *girl god*) when there is a knock at my door. I haven't ordered any food, so maybe it's housekeeping. I peep through the tiny eye-hole and see Kane's girth taking up the entire door frame. Shit. . . do I let him in or pretend to be in the shower? Are things going to be weird after last night or has he come to clear the air?

"Open up, Zahra. I know you're there. I can sense you."

Well, fuck a duck.

I reluctantly open the door. Kane dips his head and comes in.

Caed follows.

Uh oh.

I say Mio and Nyam cause trouble. . . but Caed *is* trouble.

Today, he's sporting a black eye (which somehow does not detract from his overall hotness) and a wicked

287

smile. I want the record to show how suspicious I'm of his presence. I knew I shouldn't have opened the damn door.

"Uh, hi guys. Listen, I just spoke with Khal and he wants me to email him the charts with some highlighted information. It's going to take me a bit to do that for seven charts, so is there any way we could talk later?" I say in a rush to get them back out the way they came.

"We didn't come to talk, really," Caed says in his lazy, cowboy manner.

Do I even bother to ask what they came for?

Nope, this is one of those times it would be best to keep my mouth shut. Caed does not seem fazed by my newfound silence and leisurely strolls around my room. He picks up a mesh lingerie set and fiddles with the fabric, while looking at me speculatively.

"Did you have fun with Kane last night?" He asks abruptly.

"Um. . . . . . . yes?"

"Yes what? What did Kane tell you about responding last night. You use 'yes, sir' or 'no, sir', correct?"

His voice is like steel.

"Yes, sir." I quickly assert.

Caed nods his approval.

"Now, what is this I hear about you topping from bottom and backtalking to Kane?"

Oh fuck. I'm in trouble. And here I thought I had gotten off scot-free. I try to think of something. . . but no plausible lie or excuse comes to mind. So again, I stick with silence. Caed sits himself in the desk chair and motions me forward. I walk over to him and in a smooth move I barely comprehend, he swings me over his lap until I'm face-down, butt-up, and he cracks a hand over my ass. Now, I have always fantasized about being spanked, but this shit hurts for real! My fantasy spankings are soft-handed. Caed acts like he out for blood. Of course, pervert that I'm, I can feel my pussy pulse with desire as my ass throbs in pain.

"I asked you a question."

"I'm sorry, sir. I didn't mean to. I promise I won't do it again."

SMACK!

"That's for lying. Don't give me your shit about not meaning to. You knew damn well what you were doing, didn't you?"

SMACK!

"Yes, sir. Sorry, sir. Please-"

I cut off before I can start begging him. . . whether to stop spanking me or to keep going, I don't know.

"Good. Now you're going to fuck both our cocks with your mouth and we will tell you when we are going to come and you will keep your fucking mouth shut. Now, get on your knees, keep your hands behind your back and maybe, if you suck us off right, we will let you come later."

Good grief- no wonder this man was god of war, he acted like a general assembling the troops. His whore troops. And I'm on the front lines.

"What are you waiting for," he barks impatiently.

I quickly get down on my knees and clutch my hands together behind my back. Kane steps forward, pulling his glorious member out for me to suck. I have always felt head was a two part job, requiring both hands and mouth. Now I'm required to revamp my strategy. I'm forced to use my tongue extra. . . and more creatively, as well. I suction my mouth around Kane's length and flick my tongue across the tip, before flattening it out and pressing down as hard I can. His growls shake his body and I almost chance another punishment to rake my nails down his thighs.

I look sideways at Caed, judging the probability of getting away with moving my hands. . . but he eyes me like a hawk. A hawk who is just waiting for me to disobey so he can paddle my ass again. I give him pouty eyes. He gives me a naughty smile and slowly starts jacking himself off outside his jeans. Fuck me. I'm going to combust. I rock back on my heels and covertly attempt to rub my pussy against them. I see Caed's eyes flash in warning. I'm walking on thin ice.

I refocus on Kane. I love the salty taste and smooth feel of him. I remember him making me touch myself. . . his deep voice telling me what to do. I moan in ecstasy. I try to keep quiet. If another guest walks by, they might knock trying to figure out what decadent spa service I'm getting that is making me do a spot-on Meg Ryan impression.

And I'm not even coming.

Yet.

I'm going to fight someone if I don't get mine.

Caed stands up to direct me and both men tower over my knelt form. I feel so vulnerable and slight, but also inviolate wedged between these two men. A heady, potent combination that accelerates my lust further. Like Kane, Caed uses my hair to guide my movements. He's even less gentle and slams my mouth repeatedly from the tip to the base of Kane. Tears are streaming down my face. Kane is huge and my mouth feels slightly numb from the abuse. Caed continues to stroke himself while still micromanaging our fuck-fest.

Impressive multi-tasking skills.

Kane swells in my mouth and I know he's close, but I stay quiet. I have learned my lesson. . . this time. All I know is that Caed is a big enough asshole to walk out of here without giving me release. My hands would be a sad substitute after being treated to more other-person orgasms than I have had personal ones in my entire life. I'm like an addict; I need them to get me off. I think of this when I twist my head and suck sideways as far down Kane as I can go so I can watch him. Kane drops his back and howls out in his gratification. And I drink in every last bit of his cum.

Caed picks me up, *literally* shoves everything off the table, and lays me atop of it. He spreads my legs and *binds* them to the two table legs.

Where in the fuck did he get ties?

And he sure as shit knows how to use them. He had my legs secured in under thirty seconds.

Mr. Marx will see you now.

We can laugh at my sad *Fifty Shades of Gray* joke later, because Kane has just gotten to his knees in front of the table and his mouth aligns perfectly with my pussy.

Thank you, sweet lord.

I barely have enough time to register Kane's tongue licking my folds, when Caed grabs my wrists, pulls them above my head, releases his dick from his tight-ass jeans, and is sliding it deep inside my mouth.

Did I say he had *impressive multi-tasking skills?*

I meant fucking medal-award level talent.

No wonder humans venerate these men. I would happily bow at their altar to worship them. . . especially with my mouth.

And hands, if they were allowed.

So while Caed earns an award for his skills. . . me-not so much. I want to focus on Caed's dick in my mouth because I adore the different taste and texture of him compared to Kane. . . but I adore Kane's mouth fucking my pussy even more.

"Pay attention," Caed rumbles. "Give me your best, Zahra."

An unspoken promise hangs in the air: if I give my best, they will give theirs. So I double my efforts and I'm rewarded in kind. Fingers join Kane's mouth and I race to the brink and hang on the precipice, waiting. . . so close, but I know I need their permission first. . .

"Come, Zahra," Kane whispers against my center.

Oh, thank god. . .

My orgasm surges through me in an explosion of visceral sensation. Caed gives me no warning when he quickly follows suit, his thick cock exploding inside my mouth. He pulls back so he can cover my mouth and chin with his jizz. I sweep my tongue out to lick off what I can get and his eyes darken in rekindled lust. I smile languidly. My body feels heavy and sated. Kane unties my legs and picks me up, but I'm already nodding off to sleep. The only thing that would have completed this stereotypical scene is if I had told them to make a sandwich first.

Oh well, I can ask when I get up.

CHAPTER 34

SATURN

It's mid-morning Saturday, and we are all in the office to go over Zahra's notations to our charts. Of course, Mars and Jupiter wore her out, so instead of receiving them yesterday morning, like I was promised, I did not get them until late last night. I look at the clock on my desk and note Zahra will be boarding her plane soon to go back home.

I'm not comfortable with her leaving, but she shows no signs of remembering anything and she'll return Monday morning. The guys and I have worked a system to keep tabs on her. With this new information she sent us, we should be able to glean something useful and hopefully by her return, we will have the answers we seek and we can. . . end everything.

I sigh. Like the others, I have gotten caught up in *Zahra*. But that is not her, no more than I'm Khalid Al-Zahil. It's an unspoken uneasiness in all of us and I know I'll have to be the one to finish her in the end. I'm the only one who has not grown *emotionally close*. Luckily, my curse will not allow me. Attachment equals a loss of control.

I open up the email Zahra sent me with all the charts. She has also sent me a list of information regarding basic astrology- which she named 'Zahra's BA Cheat Sheet'. Does BA stand for *badass* or *basic astrology*? One can never tell with that girl. Humble she's not. I notice there are eight attachments, instead of seven. I click them all open. They look like printed charts that she manually marked and then took pictures of, but it's all very detailed and I appreciate her color-coded notes.

The eighth document has no writing and I think she must have uploaded it by mistake. The name says 'Jane Doe' at the top, but I see the Capricorn sun and figure it's Zahra's natal chart. I print everything out and give the guys copies so we can start figuring out how the Part of Fortune factors into our curse. Of course, I want to start at the top, but the guys groan and whine like little bitches about it. Screw them. I'm the god of discipline for a reason. I have the tenacity to undo Lina's handiwork, but there must be a methodology to figuring it out. Starting at the beginning just makes sense.

"What were Lina's exact words when she imprecated us?" I ask to no one in particular.

"Stop being a wanker," Pluto grinds out. "You know damn well as the rest of what she said."

I sigh, "Stop being difficult. There is a method to my madness."

Jupiter steps in, apparently our peacekeeper once again, "She said: By the black of the moon, you too shall all become dark. Cursed to roam your creation, reincarnating until you finally destroy it. Only the maiden rising from light can save you from becoming your shadow selves."

"And we translated it as: You're doomed to become monsters of your darker sides, trapped in human form, obliterating earth with your corruption, unless you choose my pussy once and for all."

"Thanks for the summary, Mercury. As usual, you're quite glib," I say wryly.

"Well, what do you want from him? We have been over this a thousand times." Sun says, backing Mercury.

"Cut him some slack. We all know how Saturn operates and he's damn good at finding answers because of it."

Mars surprises me with his defense. In fact, this whole conversation floors me. By this point in a disagreement, we are usually physically fighting one another. Aside from Jupiter laying out Mars, we haven't come to blows. . . since before Zahra arrived. Odd, considering how her presence should amplify our curse, not subdue it. . . My heart kicks up a notch while I mull over Lina's words.

297

"What if Lina didn't mean her in the curse?"

"What," asks Neptune.

"Of course she meant herself, that was her evil little twist. When we learned that she was playing us all behind our backs and we dropped her like yesterday's news, she became enraged. A woman scorned. . . she cursed us because we refused to dance to *her* tune. And her ultimatum was either we become monsters and annihilate everything in our path or we share her- the very thing we initially refused." Uranus supplies.

"And she says *maiden of light*. . . as in the light side of the moon. And we are the dark side by succumbing to our curse." Sun adds.

"No, she says *the maiden rising from light*," Pluto corrects.

"The maiden is Virgo in astrology- where our Part of Fortune is. . . what else did Zahra say about finding balance in the chart? We have looked at almost everything. . . except for degrees. Everyone look at their chart and see if there is any correlation to your Part of Fortune and the house and planet degrees."

I look down at mine, ignoring where Zahra has marked my chart to show me the balance through the houses. I focus on my Part of Fortune. It's at twelve degrees, twenty-two minutes. . . the numbers admittedly do not mean anything to me, but I keep looking around the wheel. Nothing really- wait, my Venus is exactly twelve degrees and twenty-two minutes.

I'm too old to believe in coincidence.

I tell everyone my revelation.

"My Part of Fortune is three degrees, sixteen minutes and so is my Venus," Jupiter calls out.

"Our Part of Fortune is twenty-seven degrees even. . . and so is our Venus." Neptune says.

"My Part of Fortune and Venus match, too," chimes in Sun.

"As do mine," add Pluto, Mars, and Mercury.

I pause to think. . .

"Jupiter, what did Zahra say to you about her name?"

"That she was born on New Year's Day and apparently there is some Basque holiday of the same making called 'Altizarra'," he sucks in a shocked breath. "It's to celebrate the return of Venus in the sky."

I type *altizarra* into the computer. . . it's Euskara for Venus. I think to my mother tongue, which I have not used since my early youth- *alzahra* means *Venus*.

It's in her name.

I grab up her chart, searching, before passing it to Mars.

"Zahra is not Lina." I state definitively.

"What?" He asks.

"Look."

Everyone gets up to crowd around Mars. I see when Pluto and Jupiter make the connection.

"Her tattoo. . ." Jupiter mumbles.

"Will someone tell me what the fuck is going on?" Mars demands.

"Zahra is *Virgo Rising-*"

"So?"

"So- she's *the maiden rising* and look, her Venus is conjunct her Ascendant. . . she's the maiden rising from light. . . the light of the second planet."

"Lina let us think the reverse to her curse was choosing her or our destruction, but really it was another woman all along," Mercury whispers.

"Another planetary goddess," Mars adds, finally getting on board.

"And Zahra is Venus- our Part of Fortune to break the curse," Uranus muses.

Neptune lets out an incredulous laugh.

"She wasn't full of hippy bullshit, *bratik*. . . love *is* the answer because Venus is the goddess of love."

He tells us what he and Uranus gleaned from Zahra while repressing her memories.

"But why have we never encountered her before?" Sun wonders.

"Because Lina kills her first." Pluto states. Being the god of death, he's linked to Lina's darker side more so than the rest of us and can always recognize when she has taken human lives in the past. . . now it makes sense who she was killing. Being aware of that part of her curse made her look for Venus' reincarnation every time she was reborn. . . and we never knew.

"We have to get to Zahra!" Mercury says, panicking.

"She's boarding her flight, if not already on the plane- she'll be safe until she lands and we will be waiting for her in Minnesota," I calmly reason.

The shrill ring of my telephone jars us and I reach over my desk to answer it. Who the hell is calling on a Saturday morning?

"Hello?"

"Yes, hello, I'm looking for a Mr. Al-Za. . . Al-Zahil?" The feminine voice on the other line butchers my last name.

"Speaking, how may I help you?"

"Forgive me, sir, I'm calling from Southwest Airlines. We are looking for a Zahra Delsol. . . we are doing last minute calls and she's the only one not accounted for, but her ticket information lists your name and number. Do you know if she'll be making this flight?"

My heart freezes in my chest.

"No, thank you." I click the phone down before looking at the others. They heard everything and all share the same looks of horror.

"Let's try giving Zahra a call."

I try her cell, but get no answer. The ice in my chest is spreading to the rest of my body. I pull up the resort's

302

security cameras and home in on her room. At 7:45, she opens the door to take her breakfast. . . and never leaves. Mercury and Sun wink out before anyone else can move. They return in minutes. Their ashen faces say it all.

"She's gone. . . someone ransacked her room and took her," Sun chokes out.

I try to use my connection to trace her energy, but feel nothing. Despair replaces the ice inside of me. And wars with regret. Our one chance at salvation- at true love- gone.

And I never got to apologize.

CHAPTER 35

ZAHRA

My alarm goes off at 7:30. I have breakfast coming in fifteen minutes, but I stay in bed, scrolling through my phone. I go back home today. It's 23° in Clemenston.

So fucking depressing.

I make sure Khal got my email from last night. . . I hope he can read through my notes. If not, I can translate when I get back. A knock at my door signals food is here. Another glorious platter of fresh fruit.

Oh fruit- you will be missed.

I take a few bites of watermelon, skirting the grapes. I'm still hesitant to eat one after. . . the previous debacle. I'm sure you can understand my apprehension.

I hop into the shower and sing *Uptown Funk* horribly off-key, while dancing just as sadly, I'm sure. (This is where you reassure me that I'm a fantastic singer and dancer. Friends lie to each other like that, even if they are in the Trust Tree of Truth. It's a tricky line to walk, figuring out this whole friends' honesty thing, but we'll get there.) Once clean, I towel off and slather on the resort's complimentary lotion. Made with real shea butter. You know- the really

305

fancy, expensive shit that makes your skin look and feel like silk? I should have told housekeeping I was out, so I had some for when I'm not staying here anymore.

I walk out of the bathroom to get dressed. . . and backpedal quickly inside. Walking around my room are two. . .women. . . I guess you would say. They are tall and willowy and exceptionally lovely. . . and totally *not* human. They have an Oriental flare to their looks, but their eyes are three sizes too big and are angled like a cat's. They appear to be twins and they appear to be looking for something. . . if them snooping through my stuff is any hint. Finally, I say *fuck it* (thank you, book!) and go to confront them.

"Ah, hi?"

Both of their heads swing towards me in unison and sway lightly from side to side. They remind me of the Siamese cats from *Lady in the Tramp*.

Creepy as fuck.

"Hello, Earth girl," they hiss together.

"Um. . . who are you guys?"

"We are not guys. We are North Node and South Node."

As in the *Lunar Nodes?*

306

"Did the guys send you?"

"No, Selina sent us."

"Who the hell is Selina?"

"She's Moon."

Oh, that clarifies everything. . . not.

"Wait. . . moon. . . she's *the Moon*?"

"Yes," they hiss. I really wish one of them would speak at a time. It's super fucking weird.

I think about the guys and their preoccupation with the moon- an afflicted moon, more specifically. This doesn't bode well for me, does it?

"Ok, what does Moon want with me?"

"To kill you," they answer.

Huh, well, I found my girl god and the bitch wants me dead.

Figures.

Well, you know how I act in times of emergency. . . not well, people.

Not.

Well.

I drop the towel wrapped around me and start running around the room, buck-ass naked- even though Thing One and Thing Two are not chasing me. Remember that crazy card I have been holding to my chest all this time? I'm using it now. Except, the Nodes do not seem too terribly disturbed by seeing a naked, Earth chic run around like an insane person. . . maybe I need to kick it up a notch. I don't really have any weapons handy. But I do have my make-up bag. I grab some powder bronzer out and twist open the cap. If anyone ever needed a sun-kissed pick-me-up, it's these two.

"The power of Christ compels you, bitches," I screech before tossing the make-up in their faces like it's holy water.

They just blink their creepy-ass eyes at me.

"Who is Christ?" South Node asks North Node. . . except both say the words. . .

I lied. All those other times were never as fucked up as this situation. I've hit my quota of 'fuck-its' for the morning and I think it's time to haul ass out of here. I run to the door, but raking nails tangle in my hair and pull me down. I try to throw out a boob punch, but these girls are flatter than pancakes. And made of steel. I think I just broke my effing hand! The one I hit doesn't even grunt.

"HEEEELLLLLLLLLPPPPPPPPP!" I shriek and then stop.

I remember reading that you should never call for help because other people would not want to get involved-you know, in case it put them in a dangerous situation, too. How *fucked up* is that? No wonder humanity is going down the tubes. Anyway, it said to yell 'fire' instead- because *that's* something I would want to run headlong into, right? But whatever, if statistics tell me to yell fire, then I'm yelling:

"FIIIIIIIIIIIIIIIIIRRRRRRRRRRRRRRRRREEEEE EEEEE!"

Bitch One and Bitch Two (as I'm now calling them) do not even look fazed. Bitch One yanks my hair until I cry out in pain and fall to their feet. They study me with clinical detachment for a moment until Bitch Two raises her arm and backhands me across the face. I blackout.

I hate to even say this. . .

But I think those two skanks just won this round.

That's ok.

Just wait until I wake up again.

Petrified, hungry, psycho Zahra Delsol will be a force to be reckoned with.

MOON

I finger my homemade necklace, while contemplating how beautifully everything is unraveling for me. The white bones jangle together when I drop it back to my chest. I cannot wait to add to it. Zahra's teeth will make a lovely, and final, addition to my keepsake. Only, this time, I'll not wait until the Venus' death to pull out what I want.

No.

This Venus has crossed the line. No one touches my men. She must pay the ultimate penalty. Yanking out her molars is child's play compared to what I have planned for her. As soon as North Node and South Node return, we can let the fun begin. My deranged laughter echoes around me.

Eons of time waiting for those eight have left me unhinged. They must be punished, too. Luckily, Zahra will fulfil all my needs. Her torture will be punishment for everyone. My brilliance astounds me sometimes. For I'm truly a masterful coordinator. I have been orchestrating events in the boys' lives for decades, and those fools have never suspected a thing.

And they won't, until it's too late.

In two weeks' time, the total Lunar eclipse will be upon us. Without Venus, the guys must choose destruction and darkness or *me*. And I know them too well, they will never surrender to their shadow sides. No, they *will* choose me. And I'm going to make them pay. I'll bring new meaning to the word *lunacy*. It's just too bad for those eight. They have run out of options and time.

Sorry boys.

Game's over.

I win.

ZAHRA'S BA CHEAT SHEET

House Keywords:

1st house: the self, beginnings, appearance, personality

2nd house: money, belief systems, values

3rd house: the mind, learning, communication, close environment, short distance travel

4th house: home and family, emotions, inner soul

5th house: love, creativity, romance, children, hobbies

6th house: work, health, daily life, pets

7th house: relationships (platonic and otherwise)

8th house: transformations, death, sex, debt, taxes, mysticism, other people's money

9th house: expansion, higher education, foreign travel, law (truth and justice), philosophy

10th house: career, goals, life path, elders, public image

11th house: friends, hopes, wishes, charity, humanitarianism

12th house: endings, subconscious mind, karma, dreams, intuition, spirituality, illusion/delusion, records

Sign Keywords:

Aries ♈ (Cardinal Fire, 1st house, Mars)

Taurus ♉ (Fixed Earth, 2nd house, Venus)

Gemini ♊ (Mutable Air, 3rd house, Mercury)

Cancer ♋ (Cardinal Water, 4th house, Moon)

Leo ♌ (Fixed Fire, 5th house, Sun)

Virgo ♍ (Mutable Earth, 6th house, Mercury)

Libra ♎ (Cardinal Air, 7th house, Venus)

Scorpio ♏ (Fixed Water, 8th house, Pluto)

Sagittarius ♐ (Mutable Fire, 9th house, Jupiter)

Capricorn ♑ (Cardinal Earth, 10th house, Saturn)

Aquarius ♒ (Fixed Air, 11th house, Uranus)

Pisces ♓ (Mutable Water, 12th house, Neptune)

Zodiac Notes:

Fire and Air are <u>masculine</u>.

Earth and Water are <u>feminine</u>.

Cardinal: associated with the qualities of leadership, initiation, action, and ambition (Angular: four cardinal house- 1st, 4th, 7th, 10th)

Fixed: associated with the qualities of accumulation, stability, and resolution (Succedent: four fixed houses: 2nd, 5th, 8th, 11th)

Mutable: associated with the qualities of versatility, adaptability, and intuition (Cadent: four mutable houses- 3rd, 6th, 9th, 12th)

Retrograde: reviewing lessons/themes

Planet Keywords:

Sun ☉ (rules the self)

Moon ☽ (rules emotions)

Mercury ☿ (rules the mind)

Venus ♀ (rules relationships & money)

Mars ♂ (rules energy & drive)

Jupiter ♃ (rules expansion, exploration, new experiences)

Saturn ♄ (rules goals, ambitions, responsibilities)

Uranus ♅ (rules change, independence, the unconventional)

Neptune ♆ (rules your subconscious, spirituality)

Pluto ♇ (rules power, control, transformations)

Aspect Keywords:

Conjunct: elevates the energy (together or in conjunction)

Sextile/Trine: creates harmony (two or four houses apart)

Square: creates friction or energy (three houses apart)

Opposition: creates opposition or a need for balance (six houses apart)

THANK YOU

Thank you, reader! I hope you enjoyed the story. The second book is out! If you liked what you read, please consider leaving a review. As a fellow reader, reviews sometimes help make or break a decision to read a book. Here is a link: https://www.amazon.com/Rising-Reverse-Fantasy-Afflicted-Zodiac-ebook/dp/B07P8B6B5H/ref=sr_1_1_sspa?keywords=virgo+rising&qid=1553893842&s=gateway&sr=8-1-spons&psc=1

If you would like book updates or interesting astrology tips (from Zahra), please like my Facebook author page (M.J. Marstens Books). Any comments, questions, concerns, etc. can be sent there, too. And for sneak peeks at upcoming books, please join my private reading group (M.J. Marstens' Naughty Readers).

ACKNOWLEDGEMENTS

A personal thanks to you, for reading. Also, to my kids, who put up with me constantly typing when inspiration struck (even during an Uno card game). And lastly, to everyone who has supported me in this creative endeavor. You know who you're and I thank you. Lastly, thank you Amazon for having such an amazing platform for authors to express themselves and sell their work. You make it both easy and possible. You guys rock.

ABOUT THE AUTHOR

Bestselling author M.J. Marstens mixes romance, suspense, comedy, and sassy characters who can say whatever they are thinking because it's just a story. When she's not creating steamy scenes or laugh-out-loud fiascos, she's refereeing her three children that she homeschools. In her free time, she loves to eat, sleep, and pray that her children do not turn out like the characters she writes about in her books.

Please connect with her here:

FACEBOOK PAGE:

https://www.facebook.com/M.J.Marstens

FB GROUP:

https://www.facebook.com/groups/MJMarstensPRgroup/

AMAZON:

https://www.amazon.com/M.J.-Marstens/e/B07P1FVKNK/ref=dp_byline_cont_ebooks_1

GOODREADS:

https://www.goodreads.com/author/show/18921840.M_J_Marstens

OTHER WORKS BY M.J. MARSTENS

Virgo Rising (The Afflicted Zodiac I)

Retrograde (The Afflicted Zodiac II)

Exposed (Lascivious Littles: RH Shorts)

Unveiled (Dark Ménage Standalone) July 2019

Total Lunar Eclipse (The Afflicted Zodiac III) August 2019

The Swan Empress (An RH Retelling of Swan Lake) Winter 2020

Made in the
USA
Monee, IL